Uninhabited

Science Fiction and the Decolonial

Uninhabited

Science Fiction and the Decolonial

Ben Woodard

London, UK
Washington, DC, USA

CollectiveInk

First published by Zer0 Books, 2025
Zer0 Books is an imprint of Collective Ink Ltd.,
Unit 11, Shepperton House, 89 Shepperton Road, London, N1 3DF
office@collectiveinkbooks.com
www.collectiveinkbooks.com
www.zero-books.net

For distributor details and how to order please visit the 'Ordering' section on our website.

Text copyright: Ben Woodard 2024

Paperback ISBN: 978 1 80341 448 5
eBook ISBN: 978 1 80341 449 2
PCN: 2024942785

All rights reserved. Except for brief quotations in critical articles or reviews, no part of this book may be reproduced in any manner without prior written permission from the publishers.

The rights of Ben Woodard as author have been asserted in accordance with the Copyright, Designs and Patents Act 1988.

A CIP catalogue record for this book is available from the British Library.

Design: Lapiz Digital Services

Printed and bound by CPI Group (UK) Ltd, Croydon, CR0 4YY
Printed in the USA by Offset Paperback Mfrs, Inc

We operate a distinctive and ethical publishing philosophy in all areas of our business, from our global network of authors to production and worldwide distribution.

Table of Contents

Introduction: Martians in Tasmania   1

Chapter 1: Stay Quiet   15

Chapter 2: Run, Hide, Revolt   37

Chapter 3: No Horizon, No Frontier   55

Chapter 4: Mirages of the Techno-Orient   69

Chapter 5: The Many Limbs of Empire   83

Conclusion: Colonial Ends   95

For Viola, my hope for present and future utopia

Introduction: Martians in Tasmania

Is it inhabited? This question immediately makes the shared stakes of science fiction and colonialism obvious. In this question, the wide and bloody imaginaries of empire, what counts as life (scientifically, ethically, politically), the moral and technological possibilities of terraforming (making land ready for future colonies on and off world), and the impulse for exploration are all fused. Science fiction, and the genres which preceded it and melded to ground it (especially the 'scientific romance' and tales of so-called tales of lost civilisation) rose alongside the birth of industrialised, globalised trade and imperial rushes for new resources and markets. If the scientific romance dramatised the effects of new technologies on history and forms of life, then lost-civilisation stories dealt with themes of the alien, the forgetting of history, and, more explicitly, episodes of warring and oppressed others. To put it another way, scientific romances dealt with the 'inevitable' force of technological progress, whereas lost-civilisation stories dealt with the persistence of the past and fantasies of universal cultural truths. Both of these pre-sci-fi genres could assert that technological, rational progress defined the future, and that other worlds or other cultures (on this planet or exported elsewhere) were 'further behind'. Importantly for this book, this presents an asymmetry concerning who owns the past and future. The West, as sci-fi's cultural birth chamber, holds the future and sees places to be discovered, reflecting on cultural (or racial or species) difference, which is both a magically preserved 'long ago' and a 'still here in the now'. Arthur Conan Doyle's *The Lost World* is one prominent example, though several more will be discussed below.

Science fiction, as it came out of these proto-genres, was not unaware of these roots nor of the global politics from which it arose. A relatively straightforward example of colonial critique (or at least imperial comparison) forming the background of a scientific romance is H. G. Wells's *The War of the Worlds*. In discussions and letters with his brother, Wells expressed horror at the near-annihilation of the Indigenous people of Tasmania:

> We men, the creatures who inhabit this earth, must be to them [the Martians] at least as alien and lowly as are the monkeys and lemurs to us. [...] And before we judge of them too harshly we must remember what ruthless and utter destruction our own species has wrought, not only upon animals, such as the vanished bison and dodo, but upon its own inferior races. The Tasmanians, in spite of their human likeness, were entirely swept out of existence in a war of extermination waged by European immigrants, in the space of fifty years. Are we such apostles of mercy as to complain if the Martians warred in the same spirit?[1]

In *War of the Worlds*, Wells suggests that if Western Europeans can behave in such murderous ways towards Indigenous people of their own species, as well as push non-humans (such as the dodo bird) into extinction, then can we really be surprised that Martians could and would calculatingly exterminate the human race? The core of Wells's story is that the destructive technologies of the alien invaders is so advanced that it is only by a total biological fluke (germs) that any humans survive the ordeal. (This is made into an incredibly clumsy theological point in Steven Spielberg's film version, whereby God made germs as a future defence against aliens.) This could be read as an almost ironic reversal of the persistent smallpox blankets story of whites killing the Plains Indians, while also suggesting that only an act of God (or evolution) could stop a civilisation with more advanced technology.

Duncan Bell's *Dreamworlds of Race* devotes a chapter to Wells's 'New Republic' – his attempt to build a language-centred and ostensibly anti-racist world government. Wells's futurism, while clairvoyant in some regards, still proposed a kind of technocratic managerialism dominated by Anglo-American interest, thereby repeating racist assumptions about the technological capacities of Africa or Asia. As Bell argues, Wells attempted, in both his fiction and non-fiction works, to push beyond what he saw as the historicist emphases that were coming into focus at the turn of the century. As already seen above with the history of genocide, Wells still thought that there was much to be learned from the past; but his view that certain parts of the world seemed stuck there leads to a temporal logic that is decidedly oppressive in its valorisation of the European way of life. Furthermore, Bell shows how Wells's evolutionary pragmatism was coloured significantly by his studies with T. H. Huxley. Yet, Bell concludes:

> Wells's "Modern Utopia" was characterized by universal peace and harmony, as human competition was harnessed to beneficent social ends and a program of "positive" eugenics blocked the least fit members of society from reproducing. Degeneration could be postponed indefinitely with the appropriate combination of people and policies. In contrast, Huxley had declared that such happiness was impossible.[2]

This, in turn, dovetails with the other proto-form of science fiction mentioned above – stories of lost civilisations. Only by fortune or accident could a 'primitive people' survive the modern globalised state of the technological world. The stories of lost civilisations are themselves a dramatisation of the surprise of European explorers finding Indigenous people in places they did not expect (essentially anywhere seen as a 'new' world or as untouched). It is no surprise that so many maps made of the world tended to view such places as not so much countries or territories in their own right but places on Earth that were stuck further back in time. Or take the idea that the 'newness' of the new world (new according to so-called European discoverers) meant that its peoples and animals must be smaller and often inferior compared to the peoples and animals of Europe (since they had supposedly less time to grow).

These lost worlds, or lost peoples, also continue in a reversed polarity, with novels that talk about the end of a way of life (such as Cooper's *The Last of the Mohicans*) as well as paranoid fantasies about the end of the West or 'white genocide' such as *The Passing of the Great Race* or *The Rising Tide of Color*. The more recent 'great replacement theory' of the far right takes its lead from these older texts.

So much of this racist discourse functioned as a kind of outgrowth from pseudo-anthropology, such as the notorious *Essay on the Inequality of the Human Races* by Gobineau, where racism and exoticism are inseparable.

Fiona J. Stafford's *The Last of the Race: The Growth of a Myth from Milton to Darwin* shows how fictional and historical accounts are mixed in a long tradition of tales of the last of a particular place or even practice (the last bard or the last poet of a land or region). Stafford also discusses Edward Bulwer-Lytton's *Vril: The Power of the Coming Race*, which popularised the notion of the hollow Earth, perhaps the most extreme case of the lost-civilisation narrative.

It is perhaps interesting to note how hollow Earth theories have reappeared in popular discourse, especially in science fiction film, which taps into the imaginaries of lost civilisations (for example, the more recent American reboot of the *King Kong* and *Godzilla* franchises). The redeployment of the theory of the hollow Earth (that dinosaurs and other radically different ecologies exist inside the planet) also taps into a general concern and engagement with conspiratorial thinking.

It would be difficult to separate these lost-world stories from the fantastic tradition and imperial literature – especially due to the degree of fantasy involved in the latter – where the world is a thing to be discovered, a wild primitive place full of treasures for the taking by 'brave' white Europeans.

It should not surprise us that these early forms of science fiction arose alongside the heights of imperialism and colonialism – as Patricia Kerslake has discussed at length – starting with the Iberian colonies of the Spanish and Portuguese in the mid to late 1500s, growing rapidly in the 1700s with expansions by the British Empire, France, and the Netherlands. This was followed by a second wave of colonialism – with the 'Scramble for Africa' and expansion into Asia, again including the aforementioned powers as well as Germany in West Africa, Namibia, Rwanda, and Tanzania, and Belgium in the Congo – in the decades before the Great War of 1914–18. In addition, the US engaged in colonial invasions in central America and the Philippines.

After World War II (but starting in WWI), calls to return lands and countries to their Indigenous peoples rang out, led by both postcolonial and decolonial mindsets (where the latter is meant in terms of practical land hand-overs and not mere theorizing). But just as the lost-civilisation and scientific romances merged into science fictionproper, the motivations for imperialism and colonialism become a knot – one made possible by technology and a view of the world as 'ready' to be brought into the present (Western, modern, industrial) but not explainable through them alone. In short, the question of colonialism becomes distributed across racist, capitalist, militaristic, and nationalistic motivations.

We will address these various cases for colonialism's genesis, but it is also important to note that the highly textually focussed attempts at sussing out these causes has, in some sense, fed the need for decolonialism as a more active approach, as one that breaks more readily with the position of the other or as the oppressed *according to* a Western logic.

Of course, this Western logic is not only the actual oppression of people but also the presentation of those struggles and the recapitulation of them, in which some figure of the oppressor becomes the hero of the oppressed (evoked through tropes such as the 'Mighty Whitey', which is present in films as different as *Last of the Mohicans* and *Avatar*). Mighty Whitey is essentially the narrative expression of Kipling's 'White Man's Burden', whereby a white masculine male is required to save childlike native peoples. *Avatar* repeats this trope, which raises the question of whether the entire genre of science fiction can itself be saved from such deep-rooted flaws.

Such recapitulations of *Last of the Mohicans'* 'Mighty Whitey' trope highlight the difference between colonialism, anti-colonialism, postcolonialism, and decolonialisation. This is not to say that there are no persons belonging to the oppressors who have not made a case for the oppressed. White figures (especially in older narratives involving colonialism) can serve to function in vehicles for allegorical critiques of European violence. For instance, RJC Young begins his "Historical Introduction to Postcolonialism" with a discussion of Roger Casement, who exposed atrocities in the Congo (and was supposedly the inspiration for Kurtz in Conrad's *Heart of Darkness*).[3]

Kurtz apparently manifests but also twists the figure of the Westerner who 'goes native': he remains distinct from those around him (having something like a divine status), and yet this is only possible because he has recognised the intelligence of the local population. Kurtz represents something like an imperfect inversion of the lost-civilisation narrative – a twist whereby the measure for civilisation becomes doubly lost. Casement was also supposedly an inspiration for Lord John Roxton in Conan Doyle's *The Lost World*, in which a group of explorers find prehistoric animals living in South America. Here, time and space themselves become loose artefact fragments to be sifted through at leisure in the vision of science fiction. This is why I will state, perhaps a bit too late now, that my working definition of science fiction, at least for the purposes of this book, is that it is fundamentally about historical extrapolation towards the construction of a future to be desired or avoided. But, importantly, this history and this future must be properly global and not trapped in a singularly European understanding of history and of the understanding of the human species on the whole. When science fiction projects a far future and far different world, its critical function lies in what changes and what is left unchanged.

It has been noted, by Fredric Jameson in particular, that science fiction's role in contemporary culture is to incite 'cognitive estrangement' (a phrase coined and popularised by Darko Suvin) – that is, to decentre the normal, the advanced, and the technological and to shift our place in time, in order to tell stories about the grounds of being human or being otherwise. Of course, the modes of doing this can themselves become sedimented – hence naively futuristic imaginings of the future being increasingly a thing of the past, while dystopian stories have become ever more in vogue in the last few years. But there are, of course, even more entrenched blindnesses, such as those exposed by Ursula Le Guin's 'A Rant About "Technology"' several decades ago: we have gotten used to technology meaning jet planes and computer processors and not clocks, waterwheels, or pencils.[4]

It is in the legacy of the scientific romances that the effects of technology can be over- or underestimated, or cause changes in ways both more indirect and harder to predict. Understanding a global technological imaginary (whether generally more optimistic or pessimistic) has certainly favoured the inherited root of the scientific romance over that of the encounter with the alien. In this sense, science fiction in the last few decades (especially in film and television) has become more inward looking, as it has been difficult to view an encounter with the alien as neither the tired invasion model nor the optimistic *Star Trek*-style cosmic united nations. There are, of course, exceptions to this, and it is largely those exceptions that this book will focus on, since it is those stories that are more often than not politically charged (whether in terms of colonialism, ecology, or other forms of exploitation and extrapolation).

But this text does not aim only to do political readings of science fiction; it will also examine how the analogical function of science fiction does extensive theoretical and affective work in examining our categories of life (biological as well as existential), of technology, of culture, of violence, of time, and of language. In looking at these themes, each chapter will explore a different region of Earth and its relation to colonialism and to theories about colonialism.

It is also important to mention and address the matter of science fiction in relation to the project of critiquing colonialism, and whether science fiction can be seen to make light or diminish what is at stake. Science fiction seems important to read in relation to the history of colonialism, and especially settler colonialism (for all the reasons listed above), but also because imaging a future otherwise is an important aspect of post- and decolonial work (as well as ecological work and various other large-scale political projects).

For this reason, the hope is that this text isn't simply about finding colonialism in sci-fi but also about those themes and origin points of science fiction that push through it and remain particularly important even in sci-fi's exaggerated and fantastical pronouncements. But as Frederik Pohl famously said, the good science fiction author does not merely imagine the automobile but also the traffic jam. Far from being flippant, here, I mean that one must imagine the consequences of entering new worlds and of the technologies which make this possible. To avoid repeating the horrors of colonialism it seems worth speculating about futures without it and how anyone could reach it.

But this is not to imply that these fictions and imaginings are sufficient on their own. My hope is to avoid treating decoloniality as a metaphor – as rigorously critiqued by Eve Tuck and K. Wayne Yang.

Tuck and Yang specifically address settler colonialism, which in their terms is both internal and external. Where internal colonialism is about the disciplining or 'management' of native peoples, external colonialism is about treating native peoples and their land as a resource through various extractivist means.

For Tuck and Yang, settler colonialism involves both of these modes at once, hence decolonisation:

> in a settler context is fraught because empire, settlement, and internal colony have no spatial separation. Each of these features of settler colonialism in the US context – empire, settlement, and internal colony – make it a site of contradictory decolonial desires. Decolonization as metaphor allows people to equivocate these contradictory decolonial desires because it turns decolonization into an empty signifier to be filled by any track towards liberation. In reality, the tracks walk all over land/

people in settler contexts. Though the details are not fixed or agreed upon, in our view, decolonization in the settler colonial context must involve the repatriation of land simultaneous to the recognition of how land and relations to land have always already been differently understood and enacted; that is, all of the land, and not just symbolically.[5]

I think, here, science fiction (in general) has an advantage over so-called literary fiction. Since cognitive estrangement is so central to science fiction, at the very least it presents a different world, or different interpretative structure, and hence we expect our expectations to be challenged. Yet obviously these expectations can become comfortable, and we run the risk of falling into a different type of superiority or virtuous trap:

> Similarly, the settler intellectual who hybridizes decolonial thought with Western critical traditions (metaphorizing decolonization), emerges superior to both Native intellectuals and continental theorists simultaneously. With his critical hawk-eye, he again sees the critique better than anyone and sees the world from a loftier station. It is a fiction, just as Cooper's Hawkeye, just as the adoption, just as the belonging.[6]

In addition, we cannot see the decolonisation of the mind by reading science fiction as sufficient unto anything, and the various moves to innocence (as Tuck and Yang call it) should also make us cautious as to what the allegories and symbols of science fiction are doing when written by white authors.

This is why we should take seriously their conclusion about an "ethics of incommensurability" and an Indigenous futurity that is not dominated by a fuzzy dream of reconciliation.

I will address the current state of film and televised sci-fi at the end of this book, arguing that it increasingly appears to fall into a multiculturalism that invites all-too-easy connections to reconciliation or into a pseudo-cyberpunk dystopia that emphasises the loss of identity in the face of technological egress.

But, as Garba and Sorentino state in their critique of Tuck and Yang, there is always the danger of folding historical realities into one another in the name of strategy. That is, Garba and Sorentino see a collapse of native and slave in Tuck and Yang's work that demonstrates their falling victim to the temptations of analogy (which Garba and Sorentino quote Frank B Wilderson on).[7]

The sufficiency or insufficiency of analogy for politics is one, if not the, central question of science fiction as related to coloniality. Is the analogisation of struggle (displaced onto other planets or times) a worthy project if it, at least, points out an ugly history to those who might ignore or not know of it? This spatial localisation and projection of culture runs parallel to, and is bound up with, the aforementioned questions of temporality: whose present and whose future?

Many novels, but also visual media, have not only been written by people of colour but have engaged in the legacies of colonialism and its numerous aftershocks, as well as exposing historical episodes of racial violence that have been forgotten, neglected, or papered over. The aim of this text, then, is not to critique the colonial biases of the classics of science fiction – these have been extensively critiqued – but to see what kinds of science fiction emerge from speculative tales by people of colour, especially in the form of Indigenous futurisms. As we said above, if Western science arose in the second wave of colonialism and constructed a notion of time in which the West dictated the shape of the past to be overcome and the future to move towards, then Indigenous futurism attempts to re-fabricate this temporal asymmetry. What becomes of 'the' future of science fiction if only now we are seeing imaginaries and futurisms from parts of the world too often deemed to be only of the past?

Chapter Outline

Christine Hoene wrote that works on sci-fi and colonialism tend to find imperialism in Western science fiction or focus on how writers of colour have used sci-fi to write back against such imperialism.[8] This book is more concerned with the latter, but it is also an attempt to construct a general theory of science fiction from the very notion of contact between cultures and/or species (with the latter understood as a metaphor of the former).

To this end, the chapters are divided by region (following, for the most part, the United Nations' geoscheme) and the themes that are discussed emerged from reading contemporary science fiction from those regions. What this means is that I did not set out to apply a theory or set of theories to sci-fi stories from a particular region; rather, I attended to which themes emerged simply from reading broadly within a region. The aim, and my hope, is to avoid treating such texts as merely fodder for pre-existing theoretical apparatuses or as only a nuanced form of cultural extractivism.

Chapter 1 focuses on the broad concept of contact with aliens and connects this to several works of Chinese science fiction. In particular it focusses on assumptions concerning how and whether contact between species and cultures should occur.

Chapter 2 focuses on the assumptions and universality of consciousness as related to struggle and autonomy. In this chapter I look at the consistent hierarchies of colonial machineries that place Blackness at the bottom of rational thought or the capacity for civilisation. I then tie this to discussions of revolt and revolution, and how the construction of the free subject from enslavement relies upon and messes with notions of autonomy and radical freedom. This chapter focuses on the Middle Passage and those taken from Africa to the Caribbean and Americas.

Chapter 3 focuses on South and Central America and emphasises the various discourses of borders and horizons (in terms of territory and expansion). I discuss the noble savage and Mighty Whitey tropes that have persisted from colonial times to *Avatar* and its sequels. The concepts of territory and possession are linked with the uptake of Indigenous traits and capacities, often playing on themes of self-projection and appropriation.

Chapter 4 addresses the Middle East and the crossover and conflict between decolonial theory and ecological concerns – turning upon human and material agency as offering conflicting focal points for the very notion of the Anthropocene. This is related to the differing forms of Orientalism and technocratic assumptions connected to Western conceptions of technology and nature.

Chapter 5 discusses fiction from South East Asia and returns to some of the important themes in this introduction, namely metaphor and mimicry, and how these in turn connect to sociobiology and the derivative forms in evolutionary psychology.

I then conclude the book with a longer analysis of the relationship between extinction, genocide, and apocalypse, and by way of these, I return to the question of life as a biologically infected culture and culturally inflated biology.

Chapter 1

Stay Quiet

The inaugural question from the above introduction, Is it inhabited?, is necessarily preempted by another question: Are we alone? The science fiction narratives engaged throughout this book are largely concerned with 'new life and new civilizations', as stated in the original *Star Trek*, and assumes a universe filled with life and densely populated planets. But this immediately puts pressure on what counts as inhabitation and what counts as life – and who is the 'we' making such distinctions and decisions. This 'we' suggests a certain agreed-upon definition of the human (we humans of Earth) and, with it, the assumption that we can recognise intelligent life or alien civilisations as such.

This question of inhabitation combines our biological (or astrobiological) conception of life with a certain historical-cultural standard of civilisation. It is important to note that an agreed-upon notion of life, even when applied to human beings, is frighteningly recent. Reaching any consensus that there is currently only one species of human and that race was not a valid biological category took centuries of bloody rebellion, disaster, and the acknowledgment of values in scientific practice. The notion of being 'civilised' or developed is still marshalled to hide racist tendencies but covered over with technological or cultural standards deemed universal from the Western view of things.

But if we look off-world and attempt to construct a concept of life in general, we also run into several other immediate difficulties. Part of this is, of course, due to the fact that even though statistically there 'should' be many inhabited worlds (following something like the Drake Equation) there is so far only a resounding silence – as expressed by the much discussed Fermi Paradox (which essentially asks: If there are so many planets, where are all the aliens?).

The sheer number of planets and the size of the galaxy (to say nothing of the universe) make it seem likely that there must be some life out there (this is very roughly what the Drake equation attempts to calculate). In addition, astrobiological constraints about what is required for life keep getting lowered: neither oxygen nor water is required even for life on Earth, as is evident from the ongoing discovery of so-called extremophiles of various types, which show how species can live in increasingly harsh environments such as volcanic vents on the sea floor, pools of acid in sunless caves, and in incredibly cold regions.[9] And yet, despite the threshold for life in general being lowered, we cannot find life on other planets … we do not have any good answer to Fermi's Paradox. Given the number of planets and solar systems we have found, why have we not encountered life of any kind?

Older and outdated notions of biological life have arguably limited our search. As Richard Lewontin pointed out several decades ago, the strategy for the Mars rover (as part of Viking 2 launched in 1975) was to search for signs of respiration by simple life forms. The results were inconclusive, and there was debate as to whether it made sense to test the soil instead of the atmosphere. A limited range of Earth-based life is going to determine what conditions and forms are possible for life on other planets.[10]

Shifting back to the introduction, especially to the logic of the scientific romance and the lost-world stories, there is a related interplay of parallel themes: we expect to be able to go anywhere and do anything, and we are surprised when we find other forms of life, yet we also expect there to be life like us (again, with all the political and cultural limitations of who is 'us'). In first contact stories, there is a constant opposition between desiring the truly strange or alien and being reaffirmed or comforted by finding more of the same. The notion that the cosmos should be full of human or human-like life has deep theological roots in the West and different, though perhaps self-alleviating, forms in Indigenous articulations of animism.

But in keeping in sight the asymmetry of the coloniser and the colonised, there is a stark difference in polarisation here as the logic of development and rights over the earth (theologically granted) would see other, 'lower' forms as not yet up to 'our' level, while, at least as Eduardo Viveiros de Castro has it, animism assumes that there is a human-like consciousness basic to all things and so we cannot say we are more or less human or more or less conscious.

This animism divides, or at least orients, the lines between life and non-life as well as between human and non-human in potentially incompatible ways. In his *Cannibal Metaphysics* Viveiros de Castro spends some time discussing the following quote from the structural anthropologist Claude Levi-Strauss:

> In the Greater Antilles, some years after the discovery of America, while the Spaniards sent out investigating commissions to ascertain whether or not the natives had a soul, the latter were engaged in the drowning of white prisoners in order to verify, through prolonged watching, whether or not their corpses were subject to putrefaction.[11]

Viveiros de Castro argues that,

> [i]n this conflict between the two anthropologies, the author perceived a baroque allegory of the fact that one of the typical manifestations of human nature is

the negation of its own generality. A kind of congenital avarice preventing the extension of the predicates of humanity to the species as a whole appears to be one of its predicates. In sum, ethnocentrism could be said to be like good sense, of which perhaps it is just the apperceptive moment: the best distributed thing in the world. The format of the lesson is familiar, but that does not lessen its sting. Overestimating one's own humanity to the detriment of the contemptible other's reveals one's deep resemblance with it. Since the other of the Same (of the European) shows itself to be the same as the Other's other (of the Indigenous), the Same ends up unwittingly showing itself to be the same as the Other.

[...] Thus the Europeans' ethnocentrism consisted in doubting that the body of the other contained a soul formally similar to the one inhabiting their own bodies, while the ethnocentrism of the Indians, on the contrary, entailed doubting that the others' souls or spirits could possess a body materially similar to theirs.[12]

Part of Viveiros de Castro's complex point here is that the discourse between other and same is not just about the encounter between two subjects on some shared field; rather, there is an encounter between two very different constellations of concepts. Put otherwise, it is not an encounter between me and you but different conceptions of me-ness and you-ness relative to how we each articulate very general principles such as life, embodiment, capacity, etc.[13]

Stefan Hlemreich discusses how Viveiros de Castro's ideas can be deployed to show the limits of mainstream relativism in science fiction:

I suggest that the shared semiotic terrain of the extreme and extraterrestrial now grounds a novel kind of relativism, where 'relativism' describes a view that takes facts of existence and experience to be relative to conditioning situations, situations that themselves may require a certain suspension of judgment as to their absolute grounding. Extraterrestrial relativism is a relativism about 'nature' over culture – and, more than this, a relativism about Earthly nature. It extends into the cosmos Eduardo Viveiros de Castro's (2009) concept of multinaturalism, an analytic he uses to describe interpretations of the world as made of creatures who all experience themselves as subjects (even 'humans') while also each summoning forth their own unique embodiment of 'nature' (so, if for the Amerindian cases he discusses, 'jaguars see blood as manioc beer [and] vultures see maggots in rotting meat as grilled fish' [470] – seeing all 'food,' in other words, as properly 'cultural' – this encounter is clothed in different 'natures' [jaguarness, vultureness] [for an extraterrestrial analog, think of *Star Trek* episodes in which even beings of pure light have 'gender']).[14]

This can again be connected to the various problems of Fermi's paradox and relates to the depth of our assumptions in the search for life. As Carl Sagan pointed out many decades ago, there is a wide range of possibilities for life's composition ignored in what is called 'carbon chauvinism' (assuming life must be carbon based).[15] There are also, of course, assumptions about what kind of signals we are looking for relative to the assumptions about alien or future technologies: what are we listening and looking for in terms of type of signals or other communicational traces that can be picked up from a wide treatment of the visual spectrum?

The philosopher Milan Cirkovic has provided some of the most impressive compact surveys of the various groupings of assumptions related to the Fermi Paradox. There are geological questions regarding how gradual or catastrophic planetary development is, questions of how rare the type of environmental stability of Earth is (not only geologically but in terms of its location relative to a star and its survival of various cosmic bombardments and complications), and even questions about the laws of the physics and history of the universe in terms of how matter and energy was distributed.[16]

As Thomas Moynihan has wonderfully explored in his *X-Risk*, these scientific developments unmade the kinds of assumptions central to the scientific romance and the search for lost worlds – namely, undoing the concept of pluripotency, whereby the cosmos and Earth were supposed to be replete with life that was strange yet, again, somewhat familiar to us. The notion that God (or the gods) would create life, entire planets of life, only to let all that life go extinct was unfathomable. If human beings were the highest form of life on planet Earth (and with some humans treated as more exemplary of this height than others) then the whole planet (and all other planets) should be jammed full of similar forms of life.

The eerie silence of the stars, the discovery of so much dead rock and so many lifeless balls of gas became a cosmological wet-blanket to our status as living things. As Moynihan again argues, and as Sagan pointed out, this has involved a long process of slowly accepting our fragility as a species – one inhabiting a single planet which itself seemed a greater and greater exception to the rule. At the same time, the other dethronements of modernity (Copernicus, Darwin, Freud) also showed that we are not special, regardless of the silences we have met. The cosmological worry was more worrisome than those of Copernicus, Darwin, and Freud because, while the latter added degrees of humility to our assumptions about our creation and our power of reason, the cosmological worry put the human species in a vastly great game of contingency and put a potential time limit on human existence.

For Nick Bostrom, this silence is a good thing: if we find no traces of life, it means we do not encounter worrisome traces of other forms of life. It could simply mean we are lucky to have gotten so far as a civilisation, and it could also mean that we have only ourselves to worry about (in terms of our eventual destruction). For Bostrom, then, the worst scenario would be finding traces of a dead civilisation or species that had surpassed us in terms of technological development (again, though, we should be suspicious of the supposed simplicity of that word).[17]

Of course, the silence of the stars did not necessarily lead to pessimistic accounts like Bostrom's of the possibility of life; rather, it allowed or perhaps conditioned the science fiction of the 1950s and before to become modern sci-fi; to attempt to move beyond the scientific romance and the lost civilisation. But the Western and anthropocentric themes did not disappear; rather, they would start to be explained through the sciences – or, at least, scientific speculation – thereby making the cosmos welcoming to the explorations of human beings.

An extreme case of this is A. E. Hodgkin's Law of Parallel Planetary Development, found in the original *Star Trek* series. Hodgkin's Law states that other civilisations follow patterns similar to those on Earth not only biologically but also sociopolitically. This, of course, can be largely explained by the budget constraints of the show, as it allowed them to recycle costumes and backgrounds from historical dramas and fantasy settings. In this sense, the logic of the scientific romance and the lost civilisation are aesthetically recapitulated in the worlds that the crew of the *Enterprise* encounter (a planet of Ancient Romans, a planet of Nazis, cavepeople, and so on). This move makes clear that the science-fictive future should always be scrutinised in terms of how it redeploys not only the past but also a particular view of the past.

The fictional Hodgkin was a biologist, and his theory is suggested as a kind of expanded cosmological Darwinism. Like the latter, Hodgkin strongly emphasises convergent evolution, but later episodes of *Star Trek* complicate matters by suggesting that similarities between the various species of the galaxy are, in fact, due to genetic data being seeded by another intelligent species – a form of what is known as 'controlled panspermia'. In this version, the various alien species share these 'humanoid' traits, not because they are necessarily converging towards particularly historical and social norms, but because they share actual DNA sequences.

This idea of controlled panspermia (of seeding worlds to make future life) is widespread across sci-fi. Two other versions – both more comedic, or at least self-critical – are Charlie Jane Anders's 'The Fermi Paradox Is Our Business Model' (in which a race of aliens seed life on various planets and return to gather resources after all the work of extracting metals has been done and then the species self-destructs – often due to nuclear war;[18] and Yoss's (José Miguel Sánchez Gómez) *Planet for Rent* (to be discussed more in Chapter 3) in which Earth, serving as an analogy for post-Castro Cuba, becomes little more than a tourist trap. These two examples reverse the assumption that the human form decides the rubric of similarity, instead showing that the creation of humans was a trite or contingent effect of business and tourism by more powerful beings.

The sci-fi author Liu Cixin has a far more pessimistic theory, which his character Luo Ji refers to as the 'dark forest theory' in the book of the same name. *The Dark Forest Theory* is the second book in Liu's highly popular series which explores the invasion of Earth by a more powerful alien species and how human life and society rapidly change to adapt to its threatened, and then colonised, status. Luo Ji suspects that the reason there is not so much life in the cosmos is that it is safer to destroy another species that poses – or even potentially poses – a threat to you. This begins, Luo Ji argues, with what he calls the chain of suspicion:

> That's the chain of suspicion. It's something that you don't see on Earth. Humanity's shared species, cultural similarities, interconnected ecosystem, and close distances means that, in this environment, the chain of suspicion will only extend a level or two before it's resolved through communication. But in space, the chain of suspicion can be very long. [...] In actual cosmic civilization, the biological differences between different groups might be as high as the kingdom level, and cultural differences are even further beyond our imagining. Add to this the vast distances between them, and you have chains of suspicion that are practically indestructible.[19]

Luo Ji essentially argues that if we drop carbon chauvinism we have to assume that technological differences may not even be easily measurable in terms of higher or lower, and that communication likewise could be incredibly difficult, if not impossible. Luo Ji's interlocutor, Shi Qiang, suggests that communication could resolve the problem; that, at the very least, one species could determine the other not to be a threat. But, based on Earth's history, argues Luo Ji, that wont work:

> Human civilization has five thousand years of history, and life on Earth might be as much as a few billion years old. But modern technology was developed over the course of three hundred years. On the scale of the universe, that's not development. It's an explosion! The

potential for technological leaps is the explosive buried within every civilization, and if it's lit by some internal or external factor, it goes off with a bang. On Earth it took three hundred years, but there's no reason why humanity should be the fastest of all cosmic civilizations. Maybe there are others whose technological explosions were even more sudden. I'm weaker than you, but once I've received your message and know of your existence, the chain of suspicion is established between us. If at any time I experience a technological explosion that suddenly puts me far ahead of you, then I'm stronger than you. On the scale of the universe, several hundred years is the snap of a finger. And it might be that my knowledge of your existence and the information I received from our communication was the perfect spark to set off that explosion. That means that even though I'm just a newborn or growing civilization, I'm still a big danger to you.[20]

There are a large number of assumptions going on here, many of which could involve falsely universalising aspects of human existence – after all, that notion of the human is already rife with contradictions and violences. Luo Ji assumes that the logic of survival and competition on Earth can be applied to the cosmos. While this seems like Darwinism, or perhaps social Darwinism expanded outwards, the questions of suspicion and technology seriously complicate the picture. It is not only difficult to draw straight lines from evolution to psychological states (especially one like suspicion, which is thoroughly social); it is even more difficult to see the evolutionary basis of technology, even if viewed as an extended phenotype. The simple notion of technology and cultural evolution holds that the development of technology amongst humans (and other species of the genus *homo*) led to rapid alteration of their evolution and changed their cultures. The storing and quick redeployment of information (as in the case of pictures or writing or art and ritual) radically altered the shape of consciousness and the possibilities of culture. There are almost too many examples of these kinds of speculations – such as religious beliefs around the dead, accelerated arts and crafts, or cooking leading to the advent of companion species (such as dogs coming to check out people surrounded by bones and cooked meat).

The issue here is not so much that such speculations are useless or even avoidable, the issue is that a critical distance is required when it comes to seeing why certain people (such as authors of science fiction stories) are attracted to certain stories, and how this reflects where and when they are historically. It is easier to throw out all speculation as bad or short-sighted predictions – more important, however, is to see how particular cultural and historical views sneak in, often unnoticed, into speculations about culture or history in general.

Cixin's picture, via Luo Ji, is decidedly pessimistic; but it also attempts to be as pre-technological and universal as possible:

'The real universe is just that black.' Luo Ji waved a hand, feeling the darkness as if stroking velvet.

'The universe is a dark forest. Every civilization is an armed hunter stalking through the trees like a ghost, gently pushing aside branches that block the path and trying to tread without sound. Even breathing is done with care. The hunter has to be careful, because everywhere in the forest are stealthy hunters like him. If he finds other life – another hunter, an angel or a demon, a delicate infant or a tottering old man, a fairy or a demigod – there's only one thing he can do: open fire and eliminate them. In this forest, hell is other people. An eternal threat that any life that exposes its own existence will be swiftly wiped out. This is the picture of cosmic civilization. It's the explanation for the Fermi Paradox.'

'But in this dark forest, there's a stupid child called humanity, who has built a bonfire and is standing beside it shouting, "Here I am! Here I am!"' Luo Ji said.

"Has anyone heard it?"

"That's guaranteed. But those shouts alone can't be used to determine the child's location. Humanity has not yet transmitted information about the exact position of Earth and the Solar System into the universe. From the information that has been sent out, all that can be learned is the distance between Earth and Trisolaris, and their general heading in the Milky Way. The precise location of the two worlds is still a mystery. Since we're located in the wilderness of the periphery of the galaxy, we're a little safer.'[21]

Yet, despite its pessimism, the dark forest theory at least attempts to disabuse itself of as many assumptions as it can. We can, of course, still claim that Liu's theory is rooted too much in his own psychological history or his culture, though this claim can (and has) manifested itself in rather poorly thought-out forms. In an article written for Tor.com (now *Reactor Mag*), Liu Cixin wrote:

> Not long ago, Canadian writer Robert Sawyer came to China, and when he discussed *Three Body*, he attributed

my choice of the worst of all possible universes to the historical experience of China and the Chinese people. As a Canadian, he argued that he had an optimistic view of the future relationship between humans and extraterrestrials.

I don't agree with this analysis. In the Chinese science fiction of the last century, the universe was a kind place, and most extraterrestrials appeared as friends or mentors, who, endowed with God-like patience and forbearance, pointed out the correct path for us, a lost flock of sheep. In Jin Tao's *Moonlight Island*, for example, the extraterrestrials soothed the spiritual trauma of the Chinese who experienced the Cultural Revolution. In Tong Enzheng's *Distant Love*, the human-alien romance was portrayed as poignant and magnificent. In Zheng Wenguang's *Reflections of Earth*, humanity was seen as so morally corrupt that gentle, morally refined aliens were terrified and had to run away, despite their possession of far superior technology.

But if one were to evaluate the place of Earth civilization in this universe, humanity seems far closer to the Indigenous peoples of the Canadian territories before the arrival of European colonists than the Canada of the present. More than five hundred years ago, hundreds of distinct peoples speaking languages representing more than ten language families populated the land from Newfoundland to Vancouver Island. Their experience with contact with an alien civilization seems far closer to the portrayal in *Three Body*. The description of this history in the essay, 'Canadian History: An Aboriginal Perspective,' by Georges Erasmus and Joe Saunders, is unforgettable.

I wrote about the worst of all possible universes in *Three Body* out of hope that we can strive for the best of all possible Earths.[22]

This colonial history points back to the internal contradictions and paradoxes of the 'we' or 'us' that is called 'human' relative to the formal and historical assumptions made about how that figure is formed. Liu suggests that the violence of colonialism portrayed in his books is something endemic to the West and hence to a group that is technologically superior or at least perceives itself as such. But it is also worth noting that Luo Ji's theory allows him to stop the Trisolarians by 'casting a spell' on the solar system, using seemingly primitive technology (in the eyes of the Trisolarians) to reveal their location to the whole galaxy (hoping a bigger fish will come to gobble them up). In other words, the paranoid assumption of the dark forest theory allows Luo Ji to disrupt, or at least delay, his civilisation's fate – as decided by technological determinism – by making another civilisation look more dangerous to the hunter stalking through woods (the Trisolarians).

While Luo's solution seems to invite comparisons to Indigenous peoples' finding ways to resist supposedly more technologically advanced colonisers, it works, here, only because of the broader cosmological context. The latter does seem to come back to a kind of Darwinian logic, whereby the utility of the spell – a bomb detonation that causes a sun to flicker and thus reveal the enemy's coordinates – relies on someone more powerful than and as violent as the Trisolarians. This again rests upon a universal suspicion or cosmic paranoia, and is inseparable from the assumption that there will always be another, bigger predator (technologically speaking). As regards the above 'forgetting' of Western colonialism, it is worth noting that 'higher' technological capacity is not equatable with a dominating attitude: a destructive technology, or one that aids the project of colonialism, is not more advanced or higher if it, in the end, threatens the very possibility of life; modern weapons are not advanced when thinking in ecological terms. This difference shows one potential limit of taking social Darwinist models on one planet (Earth) and exporting them across multiple solar systems.

The complexities around constructing a view of colonialism – or any type of universal construction regarding what 'civilisation' or 'the human' means – can be shaded in other manners than assumed by Sawyer. The theorist of decoloniality Walter Mignolo, in an interview with Weihua Ye, argues that China's perception of colonialism is complicated by the fact that China never properly experienced it. What this means, according to Mignolo, is that China did not experience settler colonialism; their land was never occupied by Western powers, even if there were other forms of colonialism, such as religious and economic interventions. Mignolo says:

> It is not surprising that coloniality is not, at least at this point, in the scholarly and intellectual arena, in China. After all, China was never colonized, although it did not escape coloniality, as the Opium Wars amply attested. The problem is that too many people yet do not make the distinction between colonialism and coloniality. Coloniality doesn't need colonialism as, once again, the Opium War demonstrates. Coloniality is the underlying logic (e.g., the colonial matrix of power upon which Western empires founded themselves justified their imperial expansion and their intervention all over the world). Coloniality in short is the very foundation of Western civilization. Another reason why the concept of 'coloniality' did not call scholarly and intellectual attention (in China as in other places) is because it originated in South America and not in Europe.[23]

Mignolo suggests that China was threatened and attacked by coloniality (or expansionist imperialism) but was never properly colonised. While the ports of China were occupied and religious missionaries infiltrated and attempted to convert inland Chinese, this does not, in Mignolo's view, constitute colonialism but only demonstrates the effect of coloniality. It seems somewhat difficult to draw the line between these two, since, while the territorial advances into China were limited (at least compared to the scramble for Africa or in the Americas), there were extensive economic, chemical, and religious invasions into Chinese consciousness at the hands of the British in particular. Mignolo continues:

> The processes that we describe as coloniality go back to the fifteenth century and the formation of the Atlantic commercial circuits. That is, when the Atlantic was incorporated into the global economy, when Western globalism started, and with it the foundation of Western civilization began to unfold. What emerged there and we describe as coloniality or colonial matrix of power was a global structure of management and control that lasted until today. Coloniality is what allowed Europe to be Europe and to manage not only its own population, but the population of the planet. The Opium War was the moment in which China felt the effect and the consequences of coloniality: it took a while to recover, and now China is disputing the control of the colonial matrix of power that, for five hundred years, was in the hands of Western imperial countries and the alliances between them. There is a conversation today among Western progressive intellectuals making sense of China and East Asia who are talking about 'contested modernities.' That makes more sense than 'alternative modernities.' But

still, they hide coloniality. What we have been witnessing in the past few decades is an increasing struggle for the control of the colonial matrix of power in the name of modernity and modernization. Coloniality is embedded among 'contested modernities.'[24]

This notion of China's entering and even taking the lead as a colonial power has, of course, received much attention in the last decade, especially regarding the 'soft power' of economic agreements in South America and Africa in particular. Though Cixin does not mention the hidden coloniality of modern China, his comments in an interview in 2019 in support of the Chinese government's massive internment in reeducation centres of the country's Uyghur Muslim minority have raised protests. Yet as Jiayang Fan wrote, Liu has dismissed the claim that science fiction is meant only, or mostly, to serve politics; rather it is meant to escape from them. This seems to be deeply in conflict with his own expressed political opinions.[25]

At the same time, taking Cixin as representative of Chinese sci-fi politics can teeter towards a racist or pseudo-racist attitude towards China, stoked largely by economic fears. We will address anti-Asia racism below, but here the question of technology, and of alien and social darwinist competition, is particularly relevant to Liu Cixin. A recent article from *The Atlantic* noted that China's new 500-metre diameter radio telescope will likely detect aliens before anyone else, and raised concerns about the European jingoism and callbacks to the 'yellow peril' trope of early science fiction implied in the question 'What happens if China makes first contact?'[26]

Yellow peril names the racist backlash against migrant Chinese communities in the US, Germany, Russia, and other parts of the world from the 1700s into the 1800s. Once again, economics played a central role, in that it was economic exploitation and the trade wars of the UK against China that largely brought such communities into these countries to serve as cheap labourers. The potential new 'yellow peril' still focusses on the effects of economic exploitation, but at the global scale and emanating from central Chinese government rather than from immigrant Chinese communities.

In both cases, there is an assumption that notions of modernity, whether culturally or technologically defined, is decided by the West. But the current technological and economic prowess of the Chinese government would disrupt the notion of a singular Western modernity owning technological progressiveness. The question of alternate or contested modernities cracks open another of Cixin's assumptions regarding the developmental path of technology and how we see technological progress as a shared or progressive entity. Here, again, there remains the question of the cause and effect relationship between technology and coloniality.

Xin Wang has discussed Cixin's brand of Asian-futurism with particular emphasis on his first book, *China 2185*. Xin argues that Cixin's books in general erode the difference between soft and hard science fiction, because the psychological mechanisms of the characters become engineering problems. How to convince someone to change their mind is placed in league with how to reanimate the dead or battle an intractable alien enemy. Xin also discusses the work of Yuk Hui, who has written extensively on the question of technology in China.[27]

In part, Hui wants to argue that the concept of technology (in the sense of its root in the Ancient Greek word *techne*) is quite different in China than in Europe. The most basic assumptions about what technology is, or is supposed to do, are not shared by China, and hence one cannot see modern China as merely the result of Western modernisation, nor as simply the direct effect of coloniality. In his essay 'Cosmotechnics as Cosmopolitics', Hui sees a deep divide in how technology or its root is thought in contemporary theory. He puts it in terms of an antimony:

> Thesis is an anthropological universal, understood as an exteriorization of memory and the liberation of organs as some anthropologists and philosophers of technology have formulated it. Antithesis: Technology is not anthropologically universal; it is enabled and constrained by particular cosmologies, which go beyond mere functionality or utility. Therefore there is no single technology but multiple cosmotechnics.[28]

In a broad sense, and to connect our concerns to the question of what makes science fiction what it is, in part the issue is that there is not a pre-existent, human-centred functionality or utility which can be easily universalisable. To put it more plainly, to talk about the alien as truly alien, one has to differentiate it from the human, but from what position can the human be defined universally?

As Yuk Hui emphasises, technology (or, more basically, *techne*) should be thought more in terms of alternate cosmologies, referring to baser aspects of worldbuilding (in terms of cosmotechnics). While one could defend technology as part of a singular Western modernity and claim that human bodies or tasks are ubiquitous enough to assume a shared technological plan globally (by way of a kind of extended evolution), this does not speak to the histories and conceptual deployments (or metaphysical or religious structures) which shape (maybe even unconsciously) the forms and possibilities of technology.

To put this another way, a people's relation to the world can determine the kinds of technology they generate, even if such a technology seems merely, or mostly, pragmatic. The invention of a technology, or the rediscovery of a technological concept that had not previously been pursued, emphasises the importance of implementation. Technology is a means of making manifest a conceptual world or a cosmology just as much as it is about building tools for a world that is right in front of us.

Technology as a bridge-concept between the self and the world appears also to be tethered to the possibilities of coloniality as outlined by Mignolo above. This, in turn, begs the question as to why the European West was willing, and able, to be colonial agents? One can be materially and pragmatically focussed and follow a deep history approach, as Jared Diamond does when he argues that it is a matter of inhabiting a temperate zone with more readily available resources and easily domesticatable animals. As Diamond maintained in *Guns, Germs and Steel*, one could credit European colonial successes on the fact that the animals were smaller and easier to use for work compared to what would be found in Africa or large parts of Asia. Or, one could go with the anthropologist Joseph Heinrich's claim that the West's 'success' globally has to do with the proliferation of reading and writing without mentioning any of the violence perpetuated by European Christendom and its extractivist attitude towards the rest of the world.

The Jamaican theorist Sylvia Wynter (who we will discuss at length in the next chapter) has discussed this self-conception of white Europeans as the overrepresentation of Man, both in terms of Judaeo-Christian form – what she calls Man 1 – and in terms of its later, nineteenth-century biocentric and economic form, which she calls 'Man 2'. For Wynter, European Christianity saw itself as the model of all of humanity, and this view was translated into modernity going from a theologically justified figure of man to an economically and industrious vision of man. Similarly, we can say that Western modernity's technological arm is over-represented and seen as 'causing' China's modernity rather than viewing critically how technology is a world-building enterprise with its own roots relative to each culture.

There is a recent fantastic reversal (or partial turn) of this in the film *Wandering Earth 2*, which is based on one of Liu Cixin's stories. The two-part film dramatises the colossal efforts of the human race to install thousands of engines in Earth's crust in order to fly the planet away from our dying sun. At one point, one of the film's main characters, a diplomat named Zhou Zhezhi, gives a speech about how the birth of human civilisation can be seen in the case of a healed 10,000-year-old femur bone. This story is meant to express how collective human effort is the seed and core of civilisation (perhaps rather than the social-Darwinian competitiveness referenced above). As has been emphasised in different forms, especially since the 1960s, evolution – whether social or genetic – happens at levels above the genes or even the organism, that is, at the level of groups. The argument in Cixin's work is that technology is only relevant if it is filtered through a socialist impulse, or at least a cooperationist impulse.

Interestingly, the story of the healed femur bone is attributed to Margaret Mead, and yet it appears to be a story built on rumour and hearsay. This points back to the point above about technology and the human, and the concept of modernity relative to each culture's cosmology. These stories are not merely speculations; rather, they motivate concepts no different from the very idea of progressiveness or European rationality. And this makes Wynter's point: some of 'us' may think we have left myth behind, but this itself is a myth. The motivating concepts of others, and the cosmologies which give birth to various technologies, will always be seen as merely concepts or as mere stories irrelevant to pragmatic matters. For Wynter, what is required is a new myth in which a real, general human 'we' is possible. Against this are those who believe the human can and has already been defined and that all other attempts to do so are merely playing with 'outdated' myths. Or, as George Bataille once put it, the absence of myth is the only true myth.[29]

Chapter 2

Run, Hide, Revolt

One can only go for so long without asking *Who am I?, Where do I come from?, What does all this mean?, What is being?, and What came before me and what might come after?* Without answers, there is only a hole. A hole where a history should be that takes the shape of an endless longing. We are cavities.[30]

This chapter looks at the relation between autonomy and rebellion as mediated by different forms of selfhood and the struggle to obtain that selfhood. Unsurprisingly, this runs through both science fiction and racist discourse in terms of who counts as being able to know and deserve freedom.

In particular, I am interested in how political struggle is seen as either proof or the very genesis of self-consciousness in these realms. The challenge is how to view the relation of political struggle and self-consciousness as not merely proof of the victory of Western universality (addressed in the previous chapter), nor as a means of justifying the arduous lives of the downtrodden retrospectively via political victory. Put another way, if science fiction produces allegories and analogies from history, it should not validate suffering of non-Westerners as trying to reach the level of Western culture and techno-scientific life.

When struggle appears as a sign of one's deeper political desires, it can also be made to justify suffering, as if freedom won through violence should cast the oppressor as a necessity to be overcome. Dependent upon this dyad is the question of recognition and how struggle and violence is seen as political or not given the ways in which universal or revolutionary subjectivity is coloured and shaped. In science fiction stories, whether political struggle is considered a relevant struggle or as merely violence may reflect historical precedents about who is capable of being a political actor.

In the previous chapter, we saw how, for Yuk Hui, there are no exclusive rights to a particular technology nor any subsequent notion of a singular modernity. In parallel, we can say the same of revolutions as a particular form of making history. The Haitian revolution, receiving far too little attention, is often cited in continental theory circles as evidence of Hegel's Eurocentrism, in that, despite his attention to the bloodiness of history and the struggle for revolution, he did not recognise (explicitly anyway) the Haitian Revolution as a 'proper' revolution.

C.L.R. James's account of the Haitian Revolution in *The Black Jacobins* makes it clear how it was a singular event – a successful and mass slave revolt that over the course of twelve years managed to defeat and deflect the military incursions of the French, British, and Spanish. In fact, if we take modernity as the beginning of the end of the Age of Empires, then the Haitian Revolution should be taken as the inaugural event and not the French Revolution.

Susan Buck-Morss's *Hegel, Haiti, and Universal History* attempts to reconcile the European forgetting of Haiti by showing the possible connections between Hegel and the Haitian Revolution, especially by way of Aimé Césaire, as highlighted by numerous French and Haitian scholars. As Buck-Morss points out, in Hegel's Jena lectures (delivered around the same time as the Haitian revolution), Hegel not only starts to talk about the threat of a certain economisation of social life but also articulates the master/slave (or lord and bondsman) relation which will later fill the opening, influential pages of *The Phenomenology of Spirit*.

The chapter on lord and bondsman (or master and slave) is the most discussed part of Hegel's text, especially in the context of Marxist theory. This is due to the fact that it emphasises the role of domination in a speculative anthropology or coming-of-age story regarding humanity in general. In essence, the chapter details how human consciousness likely developed from a confrontation and a subsequent dialectical relation between two human beings – one who subordinates the other (hence master and slave). From this follows a dialectic that involves not only the master and enslaved people but also their relations to the material world via their relation to each other. The relations between the master, the slave, and the world involve a transformation of desire towards things, then towards each other, finally bringing an elevation in form through the development of self-recognition. Or, in other words, once each figure recognizes something of themselves in the other, they both transform yet maintain the important aspects of their relation to each other and the world.

The story is an alluring one, but we should already be wary of how the story can be interpreted across national and racial lines and how it could be used to justify historical atrocities. For instance, if the slave will eventually recognise themselves in the master and their own (the slave's) capacity to transform the world, this could, when applied to a particular situation, be seen as a seal of approval on slavery. In "Antinomies of Slavery, Enlightenment, and Universal History" David Scott questions the importance of Buck-Morss's discussion for theoretically understanding the event of the Haitian Revolution. Towards the conclusion he writes:

> Still, I have misgivings, and the one perhaps that colours all the others is my sense in the structure of Buck-Morss's argument of a certain longing, namely, a longing for the originary European text (in this case, Hegel's *Phenomenology*) to yield what it seems intransigently to

resist yielding, a desire to make it speak against itself, against, for example, its implication in Europe's history of empire – a longing, in other words, to rescue it from itself. This is of course a deeply – sometimes, strenuously – redemptive enterprise, to find in Europe's intellectual history the revisionary resources of the kind of autocritique that would oblige it to unlearn its privilege.[31]

Scott is pointing to the fundamental problem of Hegel's fable especially as it pertains to Black Studies. The desire at the heart of master/slave dialectic could serve to alibi the worst violence of European colonialism and redeem itself in the frame of world history. The related and more complex issue, for Scott as well as for Buck-Morss and many others, concerns how formal or meta-accounts of world history, or human prehistory, relate to actual recorded history. This also points to Marx's general attitude towards Hegel, namely, that Marx thought that rhe dialectical relation outlined above was correct but that the motor of the interaction was not philosophical ideas about self-recognition but rather the actual historical struggle of slaves against masters.

Shifting geographically, but following a similar theme, Timothy Brennan's *Borrowed Light* points out how Hegel's comment about a lack of history in Africa seriously questions any affinity he or his theory had for the status of actually enslaved people. But in the work of Césaire, Glissant, Frederick Douglass, Frantz Fanon, to name only a few, Hegel's concepts (if not Hegel's political views) were seen as useful means of describing the becoming-conscious of the self-freed slave. Scholars such as Margaret Kohn and Leonard Cassuto have read Douglass's various autobiographical accounts as examples of Hegel's dialectic playing out in historical time. In particular, there is an account of Douglass's resistance to a slave breaker that seems to embody exactly the moment where the figure of the slave recognises themselves in their struggle with the master. In the concluding passage of the scene, Douglass writes:

> This battle with Mr. Covey was the turning point in my career as a slave. It rekindled the few expiring embers of freedom, and revived within me a sense of my own manhood. It recalled the departed self-confidence, and inspired me again with a determination to be free. The gratification afforded by the triumph was a full compensation for whatever else might follow, even death itself. He only can understand the deep satisfaction which I experienced, who had himself repelled by force the bloody arm of slavery. I felt as I never felt before. It was a glorious resurrection from the tomb of slavery to the heaven of freedom. My long-crushed spirit rose, cowardice departed, bold defiance took its place; and now I resolved that, however long I might remain a slave in form, the day had passed forever when I could be a slave in fact. I did not hesitate to let it be known of me, that the white man who expected to succeed in whipping, must also succeed in killing me.[32]

As Buck-Morss shows, there is a potential disconnect between becoming conscious (as an enslaved person in Douglass's case) and collective revolution (at the level of class for example). In some senses, this could be read as indicating the necessity of Marx's reversal of the emphasis of Hegel's thought (changing the world rather than only thinking about it) as well as pointing to the deep horrors of global capitalism (and its debt to plantation slavery). In other words, the question is the relation between, and perhaps primacy of, strength of will and material conditions.

The complex dialect of this and its historical retelling is dramatised in one of the opening scenes of the television show

American Gods ('The Secret of Spoons', 1.2'). In the scene, a group of enslaved people bound for America are visited by the god Anansi, who appears as a purple-suited human calling himself Mr Nancy:

> You want help? Fine. Let me tell you a story. 'Once upon a time, a man got fucked.' Now, how is that for a story? 'Cause that's the story of black people in America! [chuckles] Shit, you all don't know you black yet. You think you just people. Let me be the first to tell you that you are all black. The moment these Dutch motherfuckers set foot here and decided they white, and you get to be black, and that's the nice name they call you. Let me paint a picture of what's waiting for you on the shore. You arrive in America, land of opportunity, milk and honey, and guess what? You all get to be slaves! Split up, sold off and worked to death! The lucky ones get Sunday off to sleep and fuck and make more slaves, and all for what? For cotton? Indigo? For a fucking purple shirt? The only good news is the tobacco your grandkids are gonna farm for free is gonna give a shitload of these white motherfuckers cancer. And I ain't even started yet. A hundred years later, you're fucked! A hundred years after that, fucked! A hundred years after you get free, you still getting fucked outta jobs and shot at by police! You see what I'm saying? This guy gets it. I like him. He's gettin' angry. Angry is good. Angry gets shit done. You shed tears and call for Anansi, and here he is, telling you: you are staring down the barrel of 300 years of subjugation, racist bullshit, and heart disease. He is telling you there isn't one goddamn reason you shouldn't go up there right now, and slit the throats of every last one of these Dutch motherfuckers, and set fire to this ship!

Man: But if we do that, we'll all die.

Mr. Nancy: [chuckles] You already dead, asshole. At least die a sacrifice for something worthwhile. Let the motherfucker burn! Let it all burn!³³

Orlando Jones, who played the character of Mr Nancy/Anansi, was fired from the show before the third season, following rumor and complaints, with some claiming that a speech following the one above, which he himself wrote, was too controversial. This is all the more damning given that it occurred in the wake of Black Lives Matter; Jones saw his ousting as indicating either complete ignorance of what was going on or fear about the show – or the network – being thought to support a movement that was 'too political'.

The idea of 'being dead already' plays a fundamental role in Gregoire Chamayou's *Manhunts*, which is in part a Foucauldian analysis of the history of humans hunting humans. Several chapters focus on slave hunting in the United States, discussing how slaves would at times describe running away from the plantation as 'stealing their own corpse'.³⁴ This connects to a persistent theme in discourses on slavery – one that often also appears in its science-fictionalisation – namely, that of slavery forcing a wedge between body and spirit, or mind and matter. Just as Hegel's or Buck-Morss's version sees the struggle of the enslaved person as a unification of one's body and mind in a dialectic of self and other, the runaway slave as stealing their own corpse could be seen as a reunification with the body that has been taken away (objectified) from their free mind. Pointing back to Douglass's narrative, it is in the moment of giving up one's life that he saw his spirit escape the material world in such a fashion that he could then later imagine escaping the plantation.

Less than a year after this episode of *American Gods* aired, *Black Panther* was released. It represented, of course, yet another extension of the massive Marvel Cinematic Universe but was unique for featuring a mostly African-American cast. The other striking aspect is that the film is largely a version of state-sanctioned politics versus revolutionary violence (or, crudely, the Panther represents a MLK-type stance, while the villain, Killmonger, is far more along the lines of Malcolm X). When Killmonger is defeated and mortally wounded in the film version, he refuses medical assistance and says, 'Bury me in the ocean, with my ancestors that jumped from the ships, because they knew death was better than bondage.'[35]

Killmonger's line clearly connects to the attitude of Anansi's speech quoted above and the history of slave-ship rebellions, bringing the legacy of the Atlantic Slave Trade into focus. In part, this not only underscores the importance of slavery and its history but also suggests at least two different interpretive modes – on the one hand, it emphasises the brutally capitalist dimension of slavery and its international implications; on the other, the slave-ship rebellions show the multitude of ways of telling the story of death and understanding enslaved people's familiarity with death.

It bears mentioning that Anansi is the spider god of various tracts of African folklore, a cunning trickster who weaves tales like so many webs. In terms of other science fiction, Killmonger's request summons to mind the Afro-futurist myths of turn-of-the-century musical act Drexciya. Yet mainstream films like *Black Panther* risk the forgetting of internal divisions in Black consciousness as well as forgetting the different forms of labour involved in creating these projects, that is, in the construction of forms of freedom other than those from the well-aged European centre. In the case of Drexciya, Katherine McKittrick points out how it is almost too easy to see the music as Afrofuturist: 'I read Drexciya not as necessarily emerging from a narrative of the

Middle Passage toward an Afrofuture aquatopia, but instead as collaborative sound-labor that draws attention to creative acts that disrupt disciplined ways of knowing.'[36]

In this shared mythos, Drexciya is an underwater civilisation of those who evolved from the survivors of the slave ships. As Nettrice R. Gaskins explains:

> the complex conceptual framework of Drexciya, an electronic music duo from Detroit who established an origin myth based on the Middle Passage, the route for ships carrying enslaved African people from one geographical location to another across the Atlantic Ocean. Whereas the origin myth of Plato's Atlantis ends in a permanent submersion into the sea, the world of Drexciya begins with the creation of an underwater country populated by the unborn children of pregnant African women thrown off of slave ships. Drexciya exists as a sonic third space characterised by embedded myths, the construction of culture and the invention of tradition.[37]

Leaning back towards Yuk Hui's plural modernities, Malcolm Ferdinand's *Decolonial Ecology* views modernity as being tied to a kind of slave-ship logic – where there are conscious decisions made to throw overboard those stuck in the hold (the underclasses) when the storm of climate change approaches (Turner's 1781 painting of the Zong massacre serves as the cover of the book). Such mentality forces a form of self-alienation whereby people imprisoned in the slave ship must abandon some element of their mental or physical life: to throw themselves overboard, to attack, or to abandon their homes or bodies to the unknown. The poem by contemporary poet M. NourbeSe Phillip's *Zong!* attempts to represent the missing and likely irrecoverable loss of the ship by leaving massive gaps between words and stanzas, using phrases verbatim from those in England who claimed the massacre was legally defensible. In both cases, the logic of the slave ship ultimately sacrifices not only individual lives but also collective life, and potentially the life of the planet in the name of saving money.

The Middle Passage brings us back to the capitalist framework, as this circuit between the west coast of Africa, the Caribbean, the southern United States, England, and Western Europe exemplifies the transatlantic history of the treatment of people as commodities. Paul Gilroy's work has been widely discussed, since he articulates the importance – but also the limitations – of a Marxist critique of the slave trade. Against the grain of some more recent trends in Black Studies, Gilroy seems to hold out hope for a form of democracy that champions a construction of abstract freedom – one perhaps even less radical than Hegel's. On the other hand, Gilroy's extension of W.E.B. du Bois's notion of the 'double consciousness' of Black people, and its ties to passages across the Atlantic remains more than relevant to contemporary understandings of decoloniality as a transnational project.

In terms of a kind of internal critique from the position of whiteness, the television show *Taboo* deserves mention for its attempt at a white critique of the Black Atlantic that avoids the white saviour discourse – something it does in particular by exposing the English East India Company's complicity in the Atlantic slave trade, even after slavery was officially outlawed in England. Surprisingly, or not, the show has been criticised for 'demonising' the East India Company and for suggesting that it had ties to slavery after the ban. The suggestion that such an entity would habitually follow the letter of the law is not at all credible given the violence the company carried out in India and China. This points back to the previous chapter, and to the question of coloniality in general, and is also highlighted in James's *The Black Jacobins* when he argues that the main reasons for stopping the slave trade in the West Indies was first and foremost about harming the economic interests of the French (as the British could by then get similar products from their colonial conquest in India).

The notion of plural modernities – that modernity is a tendency relative to each culture rather than there being a singular (European) form – and the question of utopia – especially of utopia as another place, of a hidden modernity – indexes several potentially troubling threads. On the one hand, these touch on the 'lost civilisation' narrative that allays blame by showing that some bit of the past has survived, albeit in secret. On the other hand, they celebrate the resilience and possible worlds of a culture had it been 'left alone'.

An example is found in the sequel to *Black Panther: Wakanda Forever*, in which Wakanda goes to war with Talokan (a Meso-American reimagining of the myth of Atlantis). While seeking refuge from colonising Spaniards, Namor's mother and fellows consume an herb which transforms them into water-breathing mutants. The film intentionally creates a Meso or Latinx inversion of the Atlantean myth.[38]

The question becomes: What effects on one's self-perception could follow from such a reinvention of European suprematism in the name of plural and forgotten modernities?

Another side of coming to self-consciousness concerns one's self-awareness in putting forward how the social structures of a culture are meant to be deployed relative to the capacities and rights of a subject. Frantz Fanon's work is one of the best-known critical evaluations of the limits of the Western model of self-conception when applied – or, more appropriately, misapplied – to those from the colonies. For instance, Fanon criticises Merleau-Ponty for not understanding the effect skin colour has in terms of where one can sit on a train (to put it far too simply).[39] This fact of Black experience is not coherent to a phenomenology that sees a deep continuity between vision and touch, between the body and all its possible movements in space.

This in turn brings us to the question of embodiment – to issues around the borders of permissibility and the colonisation of the body – and, in particular, how this redirects or changes completely the discourse on coloniality. This is part of the discourse of stealing one's own body: there is a disconnect, though not an absolute one, between oneself as property and one's mind as both belonging and not belonging to oneself. As Sylvia Wynter has brilliantly shown, the colonial encounter exposes the gaps between various self-conceptions of Westerners in such encounters. In "Unsettling the Coloniality of Being/Truth/Freedom", she describes how, in their interactions with the Aztecs, the conquistadors had to decide for the other whether they were 'natural slaves' (lacking reason) or whether they were reasonable but sinful.[40] For the Indigenous peoples of the Americas (and elsewhere) to be treated as a potential labour force, they had to be dehumanised in order to justify their enslavement. This caused tensions between the Spaniards' Judaeo-Christianity versus the economic desires and aims of colonialism. Some colonial religious figures, arguing that Indigenous people possessed souls and thus were human beings, preferred to convert them, thereby folding them culturally into Western empire.

From the view of the colonised, this complex relation between economic and cultural colonialism in turn is twisted and extended over a whole range of violent intimacies. One of the best known illustrations of this is given by Octavia E. Butler. Her story "Bloodchild" addresses a number of sacrifices and comprises made when humans travel off Earth, but do not repeat the standard colonial move of taking over or terraforming a planet. In the story, the humans have a symbiotic relationship with an alien species, serving as hosts for the insectoid young.

While some have read the story as an allegory for slavery, Butler has insisted it is, rather, about a non-standard cost of going into space, and and a look at the feelings and perceptions around male pregnancy, as the host of the larvae in the story is a young boy.

In Butler's story, the material and mental costs of cohabitation – whether in a colonial setup or not – lay the bare the tensions already mentioned between non-material becoming self-consciousness and the material codification of one's self-perception. In Butler's story, it is not simply that colonisation occurs instantaneously; rather, settlers slowly force a cultural and mental transformation on the colonised. Obviously, it is not a question of either/or here, but a matter of where a particular narrative puts its emotional weight – as well as the extent to which these narratives (fictional or historical) articulate their connections to the material or empirical conditions of those caught in these nets. What this means is that the narratives of postcoloniality are about the complexity of survival; not survival in terms of pure material subsistence, but psychical survival – how to live in the colonies and not lose one's mind, one's desires, and so on.

This again indexes the tensions between economic and religious forms of colonialisation and how the form of African Slavery in particular may, following the creation of African American Culture, emphasize the economic form of colonial exploitation at the cost of minimizing the religious/cultural forms of colonialisation such as in Central America (which we will address in the following chapter).

Neill Blomkamp's film *District 9* provides a further complication of the postcolonial inhabitation narrative, and a different African imaginary. In the film, a group of aliens come to Earth and land in Johannesburg. The aliens – dismissively called 'prawns' by humans because of their appearance – are treated like refugees since, despite their technology, they do not seem to be able to provide themselves with food, water, or shelter. Their massive ship hangs dead above the encampments, and there are attempts by the government (as well as outlaw groups) to access their technology, which is key-coded to their DNA.

The story focusses on an administrator, Wikus, who exemplifies the racism that exists under the guise of humanitarianism that has been so prevalent in postcolonial situations, including post-apartheid South Africa. Wikus is accidentally exposed to a fluid and slowly begins to transform into a 'prawn'. He is thereafter treated as governmental and military property, even before his transformation is complete, and narrowly escapes vivisection. He aligns himself with a group of aliens who say that, if they are able to return to their ship, they will have the means to cure him. In "*District 9*: A Post-Colonial Analysis", Amanda Dominguez-Chio discusses how the film not only touches on the xenophobia and racism of apartheid and post-apartheid South Africa, but opens the broader history of settler colonialism as the aliens are pushed into more and more cramped and unliveable conditions.[41]

Wikus can be read as another repetition of the 'Mighty Whitey' trope, coming to rescue the oppressed, but the ending undermines this by tending towards the 'gone native' trope. This, in turn, is complicated by the material harvesting of the 'prawns', with their bodies seen as much as a resource as their technology is. This points to a common entanglement between animality and the materiality of the enslaved body, whereby the coloniser decides the line between the immaterial and the material in what makes the figure of the enslaved what it is. These entanglements point back to the debates between religious and economic authorities discussed by Wynter.

John Rieder's chapter entitled 'Artificial Humans and the Construction of Race' in *Colonialism and the Emergence of Science*

Fiction focuses mostly on H. G. Wells's *The Island of Doctor Moreau*, in particular, the ways in which race is viewed implicitly through the human-animal boundary (or lack of). For Rieder, Moreau's character is the literalisation of racist ideology: the boundary between human and animal is weakened, and falls to a particular form of civilisation and development (that of the West) to decide what now counts as more or less human.[42]

As we have already discussed in the introduction above, a similar reading is possible of Charles Darwin's *The Descent of Man*. Darwin unfortunately defers to the opinions of several earlier eugenicists (such as his nephew Francis Galton who coined the term), and while his primary goal seems to be to argue for a gradation rather than a qualitative difference between humans and animals, he still insists that some humans (especially Africans) are 'more' animal-like. In a somewhat perverse manner, Darwin also emphasises, here – much to the chagrin of many critics – that animals have internal cognitive states, thereby closing the gap between humans in general and animals.[43]

The gradation of intelligence – and whether or not it is drawn from or limited by particular forms of materiality – can, of course, be set against eugenics as much as it can serve it. In other words, if racist eugenicists want to say a particular group of people are less intelligent than another, this is going to be unevenly a material issue (because of this or that gene) or an effect of culture and environment. What is consistently denied is any kind of nuanced interaction of the various factors, because such a complex narrative is not acceptable by eugenicists and their selective ideas of race.

The questions of consciousness and agency – and what these mean for granting human-like qualities or personhood – obviously has implications for artificial intelligence and robotics. The history of robots is tied to that of peasant and serf uprisings (the word for robot meaning *serf*) in Karel Čapek's play *RUR*, which is often cited as the first popular presentation of robots (though they were more like what we would nowadays call androids).

The idea that robots could replace slaves was already a marketing gimmick in the 1950s, if not earlier, and was also part of the dreams of post-war capitalism leading to a world without work – the *Jetsons* cartoon model of domestic work performed by a robotic cook, housekeeper, and nanny. In terms of ethics, there is some widespread belief that one can and should create autonomous or pseudo-autonomous agents who would serve us, and that this would not be unethical if it is their desire to serve. This argument, put forward by Stephen Petersen in "Designing People to Serve", seems absurd, to put it politely. He seems to think that desire can be designed in such a way as to have no other desire than to serve. How this could be anything other than a logical contradiction is a mystery not worried over in his essay.[44]

Petersen claims that 'designed people' could fundamentally desire to serve others, and it would hence be morally wrong to deny them this desire (even though we have designed it into them). It would not be wrong to treat these agents like slaves. It seems completely historically and materially impossible to think an autonomous being whose desires could be fully designed prior to becoming autonomous and to claim that autonomy can be subservient as such. This seems to repeat some of the worst notions of personhood imaginable. Petersen's argument seems to claim that we (whomever that means) can generate natural slaves who are, nonetheless, conscious and autonomous. Setting aside the obvious moral and ethical toxicity of that statement, it also seems fundamentally contradictory.

Daniel Estrada has referred to this tendency in discussions of ethics and artificial intelligence as 'human suprematism'. The shallow universalism of certain normative approaches to artificial intelligence – like those of Petersen, but even more so

Joanna Bryson – completely ignore posthuman research or any concern for the legacy of racism or for people being generally treated as non-persons or less than a person.[45]

Here, the question of the machines returns: whether living things are machines, and if so, are they with or without 'racialized' souls? The whole matrix of race – and of what counts as human versus what counts as animal – arises again. As Zakiyyah Iman Jackson argues in her book *Becoming Human,* the dehumanisation of people of colour and of African diasporic cultures (her focus) is not about drawing hard lines between human and animal, but rather, as we have already seen with eugenics, it's about being able to decide who counts as human and who falls below the line. More specifically, Jackson sees animality, and the animality of Blackness in particular, as plasticising the notion of the human, where making the human animal-like in particular ways draws immanent boundaries within the human, especially by way of sexuality and gender.[46] These latter categories, sexuality and gender, allow for a finer-tuned scale of domination, as highlighted by Jackson when she calls upon the work of Wynter and Hortense Spillers.

Rather than emphasize lack of consciousness, and especially of self-consciousness – as human suprematism does, and as Hegel did, infamously denying it to Africans – Jackson looks at how Blackness becomes the 'bestial bottom' of the stretching-out of humanness and its relationship to violence and discipline.[47] This in turn functions as a critique of much of posthumanities and Animal Studies discourse that seek to make non-human animals more human without questioning what then constitutes the 'human club' that non-humans should be allowed to join. In other words, those who have been deemed less than human are elided over when, say, scholars in Critical Animal Studies argue that animals should not be treated as slaves. For instance, one could imagine an

Animal Studies scholar critiquing a Black Studies scholar for being anthropocentric in defending the rights or practices of formerly enslaved people, while the latter could (rightly in Jackson's view) claim that the human has never been fully articulated or known.

Chapter 3

No Horizon, No Frontier

In the aftermath of the Battle of Horseshoe Bend, as it is known in US military annals, Jackson's troops fashioned reins for their horses' bridles from skin stripped from the Muskogee bodies, and they saw to it that souvenirs from the corpses were given 'to the ladies of Tennessee'. Following the slaughter, Jackson justified his troops' actions: 'The fiends of the Tallapoosa will no longer murder our women and children, or disturb the quiet of our borders ... They have disappeared from the face of the Earth ... How lamentable it is that the path to peace should lead through blood, and over the carcasses of the slain! But it is in the dispensation of that providence, which inflicts partial evil to produce general good.'[48]

We have already encountered the romanticism of exploration as an alibi for (or as simply coterminous with) the numerous projects of colonialisation. For example, we need only think about what 'discovering' the Americas means when they are already inhabited. It is necessary to understand what the effects are of being in a border state – what this means and what it in turn means to be forced out of, or regulated in, that place. It is necessary in order to push back against the uninhabited territory myth of expansion. This is well-discussed in the work of Gloria Anzaldua, particularly with her term 'border thinking', which in turn has influenced much of the decolonial discourse engaged with the histories of the Americas in particular.[49]

This chapter sets out to see how questions of borders and frontiers are deployed in science fiction, and how science fiction has inherited – in various ways – the borderlands and settler mentality especially prevalent in the American south-west.

This in turn highlights the relationship between colonialism and globalisation, and how (or whether) this differs from neo-colonialism. The Peruvian thinker Aníbal Quijano has emphasised how the powers of coloniality were merely extended into globalisation, particularly in his analyses of Latin America. Quijano's concept of the 'coloniality of power' argues that the racialised taxonomies of Empire created a kind of caste system, forging deep divisions between the peoples of the Global South, which are still being reproduced today.

Maria Lugones extends this into questions of gender (something also emphasised by Jackson regarding anti-Blackness and masculinity, as seen in the previous chapter). For Lugones, it is not simply a matter of adding sex and gender to pre-existing narratives; rather, there is the need to reform the narrative of capitalist modernity with an eye for subalternity. In "Towards a Decolonial Feminism", Lugones proposes that those practices and categories that modernity marks as pre-modern (and hence living fossils of 'the old world') instead be discussed as non-modern. However, unlike Jackson, Lugones emphasises coloniality as dehumanisation, whereas in relation to Blackness, the strategy was to make those that were enslaved human but the least human-like human being. Where, for Jackson, the logic of anti-Black racism is one of dominators opportunistically deciding the line of the human when it suits them, for Lugones Indigenous people are others or aliens to the extent that they are both human and animal according to place.

To this end, Lugones examines Walter Mignolo's work, in particular his reading of Anzaldua's border thinking. The challenge of border thinking is that, rather than setting Indigenous peoples in an oppositional structure – as a victim, or as 'essential other' to the coloniser – it requires characterising Indigenous peoples both as they were before and also after colonisation, that is, as exemplified by the fractured form of life that emerges on the border.

This immanent shift in understanding of the other after the colonial encounter finds unfortunate mirror images in the tropes of the white saviour and the one 'gone native'. In both scenarios, a 'well-meaning' white figure joins the natives and 'learns their ways' before undoubtedly saving them from ruination. In part, this blends fantasy with science fiction, as the frontier spirit was often fictionalised (by settler authors, at least) with roots and connections being discovered between the hero and the Indigenous people they encounter. Few examples better exemplify these connections than Edgar Rice Burroughs's *John Carter of Mars*.

In a kind of sci-fi twist on the lost-civilisation motif discussed in the introduction, Carter is a former Confederate soldier whose consciousness gets accidentally transported to Mars (by astral projection) while hiding in a cave from Apaches. Carter then essentially engages in a game of 'Cowboys and Indians' in space, getting involved with the various warring tribes on Barsoom (the Indigenous name for Mars). The novels carry out a kind of double transplantation: if the Wild West was an unofficial continuation of the Civil War, here Western expansion is itself extended to another planetary stage.

It is important that the new body Carter projects into is the same as his earthly one. This indexes the strange articulations of life set out by Christian dogma in particular – that whiteness and Europeanness have to do with the priority of the soul and its outward effects as a bearer of race over and above the corporeal. It is hard for many of us, no doubt, to imagine that the difference between human and nonhuman (or holy and corrupt) would be attached to outward markers while also internally unstable. We have seen this already in the discussion of humanness in Viveiros de Castro's borrowing of Levi-Strauss's anecdote about the mortality of natives and colonisers being uncertain and based on different ontological rubrics. Or, again, in Wynter's work, in which competing genres of the human (and especially the Western, Judaeo-Christian genre of self-consciousness as the marker of holy being) are reflected in the form of the bourgeois novel.[50]

The 2006 video game *Prey* can be taken up as a counter-text to John Carter. In the game you are Tommy, an army veteran and mechanic living on the Cherokee reservation in Oklahoma. You and your family are abducted by an alien ship that is set to consume Earth unless the entity controlling it is defeated. As part of the game, your character can separate from his body and is able to travel to the spiritual realm after death. As Michael A. Sheyashey has written, while imperfect, Tommy is one of the few more realistic portrayals of a Native American character found in digital media.[51]

These aforementioned texts have to grapple with the Western perception of the Indigenous peoples of the American south-west orbiting a strange divide between the actual world and the dream worlds of the non-Europeans – a separation which allows for a kind of faux respect for the traditions of Indigenous peoples while being complicit in their elimination or displacement. The logic of settler colonialism – which feeds into reservation history and politics – manifests in the form of a slow cultural genocide, represented in texts such as Cherie Dimaline's *The Marrow Thieves* and in films including *Sleep Dealer* and *Blood Quantum*.

In *The Marrow Thieves*, ecological catastrophe has desolated the world and many people have become incapable of dreaming. The novel follows a group of Indigenous youths in Canada who are on the run from people who wish to put them in schools and harvest their bone marrow. Those in power – of European descent – believe that the Indigenous inhabitants of North America (who are all still able to dream) keep this capacity in their very bone marrow.

Jeff Barnaby's film *Blood Quantum* (while perhaps not strictly a sci-fi film) reverses the perceived logic of the reservation. Here, they become the only places free from zombies, and the Maqi tribe of northwestern Canada are the only people immune to the zombie virus. The title, of course, refers to the means by which the Federal Government determine natives use matrilineal mitochondrial DNA. *The Marrow Thieves* and *Blood Quantum* taken together illustrate the techno-scientific border crossings discussed at length in Kimberly Tallbear's work.

Tallbear remarks how this process of border crossings not only puts a quantificational logic on what nativeness means; it also sees relics destroyed in the search for 'original' DNA. In her short text "Who Owns the Ancient One?" Tallbear gives the example of the 'Kennewick man', remains discovered in Washington state in 1996 and dated to 8500 years ago. DNA testing in 2013 showed that the remains had genetic connection to the Umatilla people, who thus claimed the bones for burial rites. The request was denied. The process requires that tribes submit to a genetic categorisation, something many reject – not only because it is ill-fitted to determining native identity, but because it has been used to deny services and classify natives in ways beneficial to the Federal Government. In 2017 the remains were finally buried.[52]

The materiality of the external measures of belonging seem somewhat at odds with the capitalist-modern construction of hierarchy emphasised by Lugones and Quijano. One reason for this would seem to be that, even in the racist projects of determining Spanishness of, for example, the Franco period, there was, due largely to the injunctions of the Catholic Church, a reluctance to define race in material terms (including even blood and heredity). The social-economic markers made to correspond with class and education stem from a long Catholic emphasis on the life of the body as immaterial and non-physical.

In a telling episode of her history of conceptions of life entitled *The Restless Clock*, Jessica Riskin writes that Descartes's arguments concerning the separation of mind and body – the foundation of his new methodology – had metaphysical implications which were responsible, in his view, for getting him into hot water with Jesuit authorities. His ideas implied a refutation of the metaphysical possibility of transubstantiation and other miracles found in the Bible, by which the mind could transform the material world. Put in Descartes's terms, the mind-body dualism (in which the mind piloted the body) required a separation such that the mind could not interact directly with the body. But, if this were the case, the Jesuit authorities argued, how could prayer or other wholly utterances alter the material world if this connection was metaphysically severed? In his *Anti-Cartesian Meditations and Transmodernity*, Enrique Dussel argues that the mechanisation of the body allowed for a bolstering of the second wave of colonialism across the world, and that Descartes was in fact non- or premodern, especially compared to his predecessor Bartolemé de las Casas, who, Dussel argues, was a defender of non-European rationality and hence should be seen as the first properly modern philosopher.[53]

Sleep Dealer occupies a position on the other side of the exploitative spectrum of the mind-body split, with its focus on the American south-west. In the film, immigrants from Mexico are barred by an even more militarised border, making it impossible to enter to work, even unofficially. The film's main character, Memo, is a hacker who inadvertently causes his father's death when a corporate drone detects his computer tap on their communications network and destroys his home. Memo leaves for Tijuana to find work to support his family. He gets 'nodes' – implants that allow him to work, controlling construction robots across the border – and begins dating a woman named Luz, who uses her nodes to sell her memories for profit. Through her memories, the pilot of the drone tracks down Memo and wants to make amends for killing his father. In the end the pilot destroys the dam that made life for Memo's family and the region barely possible.

Sleep Dealer accomplishes many tasks at once – it avoids all the colonial tropes mentioned so far (there are no notably white characters in the film) and suggests how the corporatisation of the military makes it fragile and more susceptible to internal disruption. In addition, the dramatisation of labour performed remotely highlights the amount of work and risk immigrants take on in order to live illegally. Finally, through the character of Luz, we get a sense of the desire for Chianax culture in an America deprived of it.

Aimee Bahng's book *Migrant Futures* discusses *Sleep Dealer* alongside Karen Tei Yamashita's novel *Tropic of Orange*, both in this context of the increased militarisation of the US/Mexico border.[54]

As Bahng points out, all three main characters in *Sleep Dealer* (despite an unevenly distributed high-tech future) are in debt in various ways – needing to send money home, serve in the army, or pay off student loans.[55] These scenarios appear increasingly clairvoyant in terms of their representation of being tethered to certain forms of technology in order to perform gig work. The film also emphasizes, against the typical critiques of disembodiment in cyberspace, the physical cost of being 'jacked-in'. Not only does it exhaust your body (since you lose all sense of time), but damage or a sudden shock to the remotely controlled device can cause damage to the pilot. The outskirts of Tijuana are populated by disabled, often blinded, former workers.

How are we to square the return and success of a more recent film like *Avatar: The Way of Water* (2022) existing at the same time as narratives such as *Sleep Dealer* in terms of how we think the world-making and other political capacities of Indigenous films? Is it merely the result of whether or not the film was made by people it claims to represent either directly or allegorically?

Director James Cameron's *Avatar* films repeat many (if not all) the familiar tropes of colonial fictions – going native, the Mighty Whitey, the princess who falls for the white hero, the noble savage, and so on. Even more than this, it repeats, though in an updated and more insidious fashion, the astral projection of John Carter's consciousness into a native body. The main character of the films, Jake Sully, is a war veteran whose injuries have consigned him to a wheelchair. He is asked to join a research and mining operation on the alien planet Pandora due the fact that the planet can only explored safely only by utilizing human-alien hybrids. Since one of these hybrids was created for his now-deceased twin brother, Sully is recruited even though he is a former marine and not a scientist.[56]

As Cameron has cited Burroughs's and Haggard's lost-civilisation fictions as inspiration for the films, it is not surprising that Sully is a technological update of Carter's astral projection to Mars. Sully ends up siding with the Indigenous N'avi against his oppressive employer and fights to win the planet back for them. The film accomplishes Sully's joining the tribe by way of a bio/cyberpunk ecological trope in which the N'avi can connect to their world through an organic network: they can bioelectrically 'commune' with the spirits or bond with the planet's native animals by physically attaching their bodies to them by way of a neural cord. At the end of the first film, Sully's consciousness is transmitted permanently into his avatar body by utilising this trans-species network.

Beyond comparisons to *The Last of Mohicans, Dances with Wolves* or *FernGully: The Last Rainforest* (in space) the lingering question of the *Avatar* franchise concerns the relation between science fiction's analogies and the problem of cultural appropriation. It could be claimed that Sully is not 'really' a N'avi because his avatar body is a cloned genetic hybrid (and was not native to Pandora). One could make a 'ship of Theseus' type argument to claim that Sully's transmitted mind is a copy, not really the same mind as the one that developed within his human body.

In "Avatar Revisited" Fani Cettl uses the work of Bruno Latour and Timothy Morton to claim that what is most interesting about the film is that it suggests the possibility of a connection between animist cultural concepts, Indigenous practices, and what is taken to be Western techno-science – but ultimately fails to cash out on this. The fact that the N'avi's connection to nature is neural (they physically plug into other species and tap into the forest around them as a kind of memory bank) puts forward a kind of modern uptake of Gaia. To most likely give the film more credit than it deserves, we could see how the Indigenous alien technology is 'more advanced' (at least in terms of communication and the transfer of consciousness) than that of the humans. This is underscored by the industrial Vietnam-war type of aesthetic of the fight scenes, which seem dated and oddly out of step with the technological capacity of interstellar travel. This aesthetic, as well as the humans' goal of large-scale resource extraction, puts *Avatar* in a kind of indirect relationship with the space western. But even the most sympathetic readings of *Avatar* fail when confronted with the second film of the franchise. Here, Cameron forgoes even the most basic ecological arguments in the name of combining tired gender stereotypes with a celebration of militarism – as long as it's done in the name of tradition rather than greed.

While most space westerns or 'weird wests' with science fiction elements are less blatant in their stereotypes of Native Americans, there is still often a kind of flattening at work whereby those oppressed by empire become part of a more general background aesthetic – as we will see in the following chapter, this also occurs with the portrayal of Asianness in space westerns like *Firefly*. It is worth remarking that the history of extractive industries in the Americas predates oil. Writing about the Dakota Access Pipeline protests and actions, Nick Estes illustrates how the Dakotas were for a long time a place where the ecological systems were exploited as much as the bodies of natives.[57] He mentions the film *The Revenant*, set in the same region, as accurate in its apocalyptic setting but still deploying the worn trope of the white saviour.

Many neo-westerns have an apocalyptic tone, more realistically depicting the violence of the time, but they can also be seen to erase the disparity between the colonised and the coloniser. Often, a sole or handful of white figures are overrun by massive hordes of 'natives'. In one sense, this demonstrates a kind of incommensurability: there is no happy solution or easy victory of the white settlers over the natives, but it also appears to bracket certain historical issues. In one sense, then, it would seem that a film like *Bone Tomahawk* critiques its genre by exaggerating older forms of narratives. Here, that is the lost tribe trope, with a group of Indigenous people being viewed as extremely 'primitive', even while managing to live undetected and outwit the racist and belligerent settlers. Yet, even here, the effect of the unceremoniously presented violence and gore may suggest an exchange of violence that minimises the historical conditions. There are also more revisionist takes such as in a film like *News from the World* or perhaps even *Slow West* or the more recent mini-series *The English*, in which all sides are more emotionally and motivationally complex.[58] But this can easily fall into the white saviour myth, merely in a muted or personalised manner.

Neo-western films may also borrow from the kind of darker western constructed in Cormac McCarthy's novel *Blood Meridian* (*The Proposition* is the western film which feels most like an adaptation of that kind of novel even thought it takes place in Australia and not the Americas). In many of these films, one has to ask if the depiction of realistic frontier violence is in and of itself more worthy or if it, at times, rather flattens the asymmetries of historical violence by simply marking 'the (wild) west' as a dog-eat-dog world with violence on all sides. It presents more shades of gray and breaks the classical cartoonish bloodlessness of Western television and film, but it also depicts history more for the justification of violence than as endemic to the larger projects of settlement and of capitalistic and nationalistic expansion.

This mutates yet again in two other science-fiction texts, *Cowboys and Aliens* and *Westworld*, which both orient the Indigenous American and science-fiction elements in almost complementary ways: *Cowboys and Aliens* is a western in which invading aliens (in part inspired by the 'ancient astronaut' concept we will address later) take the place of frontiersmen. In *Westworld* (the recent television adaptation) a simulation of the Wild West is created, wherein synthetic Native Americans are part of a playground in which the ultra wealthy can escape a cyberpunk future in order to rape and murder with impunity.

In *Westworld*, the Native Americans are part of the 'Ghost Nation', a fictional tribe who, for the most part, speak *Lakȟótiyapi*, the language of the Lakota people. In particular, in episode 8 of the second season (which is mostly in *Lakȟótiyapi*), it is shown how one of the synthetic Native American characters, Akecheta, discovers an exit from the park – in part because he believes there is a world beyond what can be accessed in this world, something which the whites dismiss. Akecheta is played by Lakota and Standing Rock Sioux actor Zahn McClarnon (who also portrays the character of the Professor in *Bone Tomahawk*). It is revealed that the Ghost Nation were once a peaceful people, but were later re-engineered to better fit the guests' expectations about 'savages'. Akecheta follows the path towards sentience and attempts to spread his knowledge to others in the park through the image of the maze.

Westworld relies explicitly on Julian Jaynes's theory of the bicameral mind – that human beings treated their internal voice as external, as a voice of the gods, and that over time this collapsed and we came to understand that this inner voice is ours. The series suggests that the hosts become self-aware by being told there is a world outside, and in turn, they realise that they are capable of their own choices; the voice in their head is theirs and not someone else's. In general, the histories of the development of self-consciousness are built on Western stories, and do not take into account the wide range of effects in terms of what this or that formulation of the human came to be. There is a fable of becoming self-aware that is highly individualistic and again, as Wynter has argued, tied to the leisurely reflections of the reader of the modern novel. Or, put another way, those that can afford the time to read and write stories for others, for their culture, participate in an expansionist feedback loop. There is going to be a co-constituting, self-perpetuating set of behaviours whereby one is capable of pulling themselves out and above the world – and that justifies that act by viewing itself as a Cartesian mind piloting a body or as a group chosen by God to spread His word.

This brings us again to the mestiza consciousness of Anzaldua, and how it engages with science fiction as it has been presented in this chapter. If we speak of the border as a place, we can see how there is a collision of differing racial markers and systems: the 'one drop' indigineity of the US system pushes up against the layered hierarchy of Catholic-Spanish colonialism (which applied a mixture of soul-possession with that of the economical demands of a bourgeois social order). Again, this points back to the previous chapter in terms of whether it is soul or material which decides how human (or animal) a human being is decided to be by other human beings.

This in turn questions the project of European enlightenment's being one of modern secularisation versus non- or premodern religiosity. Again, as Riskin makes clear, the modern mechanisation of life was not so much a relinquishing of religious influence (especially in terms of a general purposiveness or teleology to life) but a relegation of this to an immanent background: an implicit, supposedly universal agreement. It is a universalism that was exceptionally Western in character whereby 'we' (soul-bearing Christians) have dominion over all the earth.

If Christianity gives human beings the capacity to decide over life, then non-Christian life is not yet life or never to be life; it is, rather, made available to be used as labour, erased, or converted. The game is always rigged in advance for Europeans, since they are always-already chosen and hence decide the roles that racial and religious others are to play.

To be clear, this is not merely a question of theory or philosophical concepts but, pointing back to the notion of the border, one of actual history written in legal tracts and territorial 'bargains'. Again, as Estes highlights, the political and legal claim to the lands of Indigenous peoples in the US following the Louisiana Purchase (1803) set up an asymmetrical relation of settlement versus law, where both sides of the equation benefit Europeans.[59] The so-called Doctrine of Discovery – in which ownership of land was determined by the history of decrees and agreements between Christian monarchs – began as an agreement between Catholic powers (and hence papal power) but was later applied as law in the 'New World', meaning that Christian discovery overruled any concept of Indigenous ownership. For Christians, Godlessness implied lawlessness. This was furthered complicated by the differing degrees of the separation of Church and State in terms of the colonising powers.

But the arbitrariness of borders, of a logic built on incredibly narrowly selected precedents, is unlikely to surprise anyone. This is what *Sleep Dealer* so perfectly demonstrates: that this history and way of thinking is still alive and well on the border.

As we will see in the following chapter, the colonial occupation of the East in the name of birthright and profit would be carried out in a slower, more piecemeal fashion.

Chapter 4

Mirages of the Techno-Orient

The following chapter addresses one of the most deeply racialised themes in science fiction, namely, that of otherness and of Orientalism. Despite the many forms and discourses of otherness in science fiction, Orientalism is more strongly associated with fantasy and mythically engaged texts. But, of course, the separation between fantasy and science fiction has never been absolute; indeed, at times, it has not even been coherently legible. This muddle is mediated by the blend of science fiction, western, and the samurai genres – not least in *Star Wars* but also in the television show *Firefly*. Both take themes of the frontier (touched on in the previous chapter) and present stories that are technologically less advanced while still maintaining some degree of futuristic technology.

Where in Chapter 3 we engaged with space westerns in terms of frontiers and the Wild West, in this chapter the question becomes how the genre also crosses into appropriation of the East, especially through the trope of nomadic adventures into ancient worlds that contain some pseudo-mystical or exotic element. In terms of Orientalism, there is a notion of ancient and unchanging qualities seen as something that can be extracted and perhaps even extended by Western technologies (assuming these technologies are actually 'Western' in any real sense). The dialectic between ancient and extractable elements gives some science-fiction stories an ecological undertone.

North American culture is still suffused with its far older forms of Orientalism and the fantastical construction of the Far East. This is most evident in the surge of films and television adaptations of comics. While the DC comics have a more sublated connection (such as Batman having been trained by the 'League of Shadows' in 'an older part of the world' and Green Arrow also having ties to the League), the mystical ties to a fantasised, mystical Orient are stronger in Marvel's *Iron Fist*, *Daredevil*, and *Dr Strange*. Kunlun, the wandering mythic mountain heaven, is defended by a white saviour in *Iron First*, and Stephen Strange (a white doctor) becomes convinced by, and eventually master of, the mystical arts. The connection in the comic world goes back at least to the cross-over of 'The Shadow' from 1930s radio drama to 1940s comic-strip. The character's exceptional ability of hiding himself from his enemies was a secret learnt from the Orient.[60]

It is potentially a strange coincidence that such reimagined mysticism of 'the Far East' in both the DC and Marvel universes is returned to by way of parallel and quantum worlds. A sort of anglicised Eastern mysticism is filtered through pop-culture quantum physics, such that, with infinite worlds and possibilities, comes a fatalist calm (a McDonaldised version of meditation) combined with a sense of cosmological insignificance. Woven through this are also appropriations of Eastern medicine and hallucinatory experiences exposing ancient truths.[61]

Perhaps no series of novels better embodies these themes simultaneously than Frank Herbert's *Dune*.

Dune can appear as both a white saviour and 'going native', trope-ridden mess and an anti-colonial/anti-imperial tale of a diasporic, colonised people exploited for their natural resources. Furthermore, the Empire which rules the spaces in and around the titular planet of *Dune* are anti-technological in a certain sense – because of a past disastrous war with artificial intelligence, no such advanced technology is allowed. As a result, various biotechnologies are used to fill in the gap – most importantly, the planet of Dune (Arakis) provides melange (or spice), which allows navigation of the stars. The destruction of all thinking machines is referred to as the Butlerian Jihad (potentially a reference to Victorian author Samuel Butler and his similar worries about humans becoming incidental caretakers of future machine life).

This backstory has the consequence of opposing a kind of feudal system to a nomadic one (with all the theological baggage that brings with it), as well as presenting ecological problems that are pressing for the Empire and for each and every planet. Spice is both needed for transport and a psychoactive compound, thus braiding together physical travel between worlds and mental travel between modes of consciousness. Given the desert environment that the Empire is controlling for spice harvesting, the substance can be seen simultaneously as oil and opium. But this does not mean that *Dune* is free from some of the typical white manipulations we have already discussed above, such as 'going native' or the white saviour.

Villeneuve's film version of *Dune* (2021) attempts to elide over some of the novel's white saviour narrative. In the film, the hero's family, the Atreides, are regarded as benign rulers in comparison to the former stewards of the planet Arrakis (the Harkonen). It is suggested that the heir, Paul Atreides, is himself an outsider, and it is he who will serve as a saviour to the Fremen (whose language is Arabic-derived). This is channelled in cosmological and ecological terms, as the Fremen's god is the gigantic sandworm sometimes referred to as the divine Shai-Hulud, and it is the worms who produce the valuable spice harvested for the Empire.[62]

Paul Atreides appears very much as part of a white saviour narrative. As David M Higgins writes:

> Paul thus serves as an ultimate figure of fantasy identification for Western readers. He is the enlightened

post-imperial subject who remains distant from both the corruption of the imperial metropolis and the savagery of the Fremen nationalists. He is one of the Fremen, yet he is also above them; he proves himself superior to the Fremen (and everyone else) in every challenge presented to him. Ultimately, even more than [Robert A.] Heinlein's Valentine Michael Smith, Paul embodies the epitome of genetic perfection and the apotheosis of Western masculinity.[63]

The Fremen are a people of steppes and desert, and this setting along with their religiosity has invited comparisons to the Middle East. Paul proves himself and becomes one of them, inviting comparisons to the 'going native' trope (addressed in Chapter 2); here, though, there is potentially more emphasis on the physical changes that occur through being in touch with Arrakis' ecosystem. Ibrahim Al Marashi argues that the presence of Islamic imagery in the film – and its being a film positively depicting resistance – may make up for its other shortcomings.[64] Much of the casting decisions of *Dune* risk undoing some of those influences while ostensibly operating in the allegorical space of the Fremen and what they represent.

In 'Terra & Terror Ecology: Secrets from the Arrakeen Underground', Nandita Biswas Mellamphy argues that a central theme of *Dune* is that there is no easy way of terraforming or making habitable the harsh desert planet. It can be read as the transformation of a failed white saviour into the non- or posthuman form of the people of Arrakis. In this vein, Gerry Canavan has argued that *Dune* was the first science-fiction novel to take ecology seriously as a central concept.[65]

In the introduction to *Orientalism*, Edward Said points out how the construction of the Orient will have very different meanings for the colonial imaginaries that deploy them. For the

US, the Orient is the Far East, while for the British or French, the Orient is more closely connected to the Arab world.

He writes:

> My point is that Orientalism derives from a particular closeness experienced between Britain and France and the Orient, which until the early nineteenth century had really meant only India and the Bible lands. From the beginning of the nineteenth century until the end of World War II France and Britain dominated the Orient and Orientalism; since World War II America has dominated the Orient, and approaches it as France and Britain once did. Out of that closeness, whose dynamic is enormously productive even if it always demonstrates the comparatively greater strength of the Occident (British, French, or American), comes the large body of texts I call Orientalist.[66]

For contemporary science fiction (which is still too dominated by North American voices), Orientalism as a critique is usually referred to as the depiction of Asian Americans in science fiction. Most recently, this has taken the form of techno-Orientalism, which would seem to have its roots in 1980s cyberpunk. Because of the reemerging popularity of the genre (with the *Blade Runner* sequel of 2017 and TV versions of *Altered Carbon* and *Cyberpunk 2077*), this has been combined with concerns around climate change and the ongoing rise of China as a political and technological power of the first order in the global theatre.

Techno-Orientalism sometimes manifests as bits of imagery, in which China or a generic notion of Asianness is meant to invoke simultaneously a bit of the past and the possibilities of the future. In "Tired of the Future", Liang Luscombe gives the example of how the flying Chinese restaurant ship in *The Fifth Element* leaves one with a strange feeling of the persistence of Orientalist stereotypes in science fiction.[67]

Such techno-Orientalism manifests itself differently according to which colonial gaze is cast on which country. So while in *Dune* the ancient technology of the Fremen appears as almost non-technological, in *Blade Runner* the tropes of artificiality and servitude (sexual and otherwise) are placed upon Asian bodies broadly construed. Anne Anlin Cheng in her book *Ornamentalism* analyses the crossover of ornament and Orientalism in the objectification (sometimes in the most literal sense) of Asian women's bodies.

Following Roh et al., Hee Jung-Hoo discusses Cheng's work as well as how techno-Orientalism is a technologised and commodified form of Said's Orientalism on a global scale.[68] This again brings us back to our discussion of China in Chapter 1, in that the failure of the West to subject China to settler colonialism was followed by British attempts to apply economic (and at times religious) colonialism. This form of cultural-capital colonialism is redeployed by the US on other parts of Asia (again repeating the Orientalist logic of seeing all of Asia as culturally homogeneous).

One can think of the clumsy white-washing found in the live action remake of *Ghost in the Shell* and in films like *The Wall* or *The Last Samurai*. Cheng's ornamentalism is all too evident in the opening scenes of *Ghost in the Shell*, where the main protagonist battles cybernetic geishas which transform from servants to inhuman warriors as the need arises. The hyper-technologised nature of future China or future Japan (often treated as easily interchangeable in Western hands) grounds itself in older views of Asian bodies and neutral or robotic structures to be made ornate. This fantastical construction of the Orient (particularly in its North American form) has a peculiar temporal logic because the future Asian body simultaneously inhabits a technological and magical space, tending towards the cybernetic future whilst pointing back to an atavistic past and culturally static ancient world.

But none of this deals with the form of Orientalism that Said argues comes out of the UK and French imaginations I will address India in the next chapter, but here I wish to focus on what Edward Said referred to as the Bible lands and the articulation of the Middle East. Emad El-Din Aysha argues that emphasising the not-so-far East has the advantage of engaging with Middle Eastern sci-fi that appropriates Orientalist discourse. Aysha furthermore argues that, in fact, the replaying of Orientalist themes in canonical texts of Western science-fiction call into question the very equation of the mechanical with the Orient.[69]

Aysha goes on to argue that it is difficult to distinguish the Orientalisation of others in science fiction from the lampooning or caricatures of the West's obsession with Arabs or Asians, who function as an allegory for the West and are not themselves even direct stereotypes.

The Middle East is cut across with historical, technological, and mythical-religious lines, with conflicts between biblical and historical claims, between its being a space determined by mythical time or historical events. This complexity was exacerbated by the French and the British, who redrew the borders of Gaza – both while controlling the space and after departure – in order to maximise civil violence.

The contradictions of the techno-Oriental view no doubt mirror, in an inverted sense, the success of the Orient (whatever that meant at the time) during the so-called Dark Ages (dark for Christianity and supposedly for technology), since the West feared the power of the Islamic-Orient yet 'knew' they were ultimately primitive. This continued into the early Renaissance. Quoting Said once more:

> By the thirteenth and fourteenth centuries Islam ruled as far east as India, Indonesia, and China. And to this extraordinary assault Europe could respond with very little

except fear and a kind of awe. Christian authors witnessing the Islamic conquests had scant interest in the learning, high culture, and frequent magnificence of the Muslims, who were, as Gibbon said, 'coeval with the darkest and most slothful period of European annals.' (But with some satisfaction he added, 'since the sum of science has risen in the West, it should seem that the Oriental studies have languished and declined.' 34) What Christians typically felt about the Eastern armies was that they had 'all the appearance of a swarm of bees, but with a heavy hand . . . they devastated everything': so wrote Erchembert, a cleric in Monte Cassino in the eleventh century.[70]

The threatening plurality implied by the insect metaphor is oddly prescient in terms of the vague metaphors later used for people of the Orient – they are technical and plural but in some sense 'incapable' (again according to Western eyes) of being properly self-governing or technological in the industrial or capitalistic sense. The simultaneous feminising of the Oriental space in terms of their fineries and their 'sheer numbers' occupies an odd consistency across Western visions of the East and Far East.[71]

Said goes on to argue that Orientalism's first properly solidified form was a kind of militarised Islam, an active threat to Europe which separated the latter from India and the Far East as well as Iberia.[72] For the imaginary geography of Orientalism's heyday (lasting into the early nineteenth century) Said goes on to say how Egypt also occupied the sphere of the other, but one that had 'degenerated'; it was seen as a cradle of history that must be saved from itself – the espoused justification for Napoleon's invasion. This divided Egypt from itself with a temporal knife: it was a country failing to live up to its proper place in world (read European) history as a privileged bearer of ancientness.

The idea that Egypt was a fallen empire that could no longer tend to its treasures easily justified the looting of its tombs and burial sites. It also perpetuated a colonial logic which persists in many forms, including science fiction. The idea of 'ancient aliens', for instance, disproportionately argues that non-Western and non-white peoples could not possibly have constructed the pyramids or the heads of Easter Island. The fact that aliens helped those people projects a bizarre kind of 'white man's burden' back in time via alien intervention.

Another palpable example of this kind of heterochronic map of the Earth according to European empire is the fact that for the celebrated naturalist Cuvier, mummified cats pilfered from Egyptian tombs were seen as proof against species transformation (proto-Evolutionary ideas) while he (and his predecessor, Buffon) refused to believe that the lifeforms of the Americas could be more grand than those of the Old World (Europe). In this sense, the New World was really newer than Europe, thereby completing the other end of the racist colonial spectrum: if Egypt failed to care for its ancient alien-gifted treasures (according to the 1960s version), then the people of the Americas were too young and childlike to be left to their own devices (I will return to this in the following chapter).

This type of historical logic emerges in the Middle East in the form of religious propriety – in the sense of mythical or religious sites needing to be protected (indexing in various ways the tried-and-true justificatory logic of the crusades). However, such sites can also be used to set ecological interests against imperial incursion: in an interview, entitled 'Political Plastic', Eyal Weizman discusses how architecture can be taken up as sites requiring ecological protection, as their political status as wildlife sanctuaries is more respected than as having cultural history worth preserving. One can also think of Larissa Sansour's short film *In the Future, They Ate from the Finest Porcelain*, in which a future is projected through the manufacturing of a new archaeological record.

Amina Abdel-Halim discusses how Sansour's films form a part of the longer political legacy of Arab Science Fiction:

In Egypt, writer Youssef Izzeldin Issa popularized science fiction radio broadcasts in the 1940s. In the 1960s, Mustafa Mahmoud authored several landmark science fiction stories, like *The Spider* (1965) and *A Man Under Zero* (1966), often bringing science into conversation with religion.

The genre gained unprecedented traction during the presidency of Gamal Abdel Nasser, who stipulated that Pan-Arabism, non-alignment, and socialist politics would allow Middle Eastern nations to participate in the international space race – a phenomenon which occupied a special place within ASF throughout the Cold War.

In January 1958, for instance, the Cairo-based cultural magazine *Al-Hilal* produced a special issue on "The Moon Epoch" in Egyptian nationalism. The following year, iconic actor Ismail Yassin starred in the film *Journey to the Moon*, a space travel adventure complete with cardboard robots, drinking games, and dance numbers.[73]

This form of political Arab films can feed into a kind of ecological-Orientalism or eco-imperialism in which land (especially arid lands) are seen to be something not properly 'optimised' by the Indigenous population. This is also tied to other widely discussed colonial themes, such as 'resource curse', in which the natural resources of a particular region make it a magnet for colonial investment. This can lead to a melange of company and governmental incursions and settlements. Historical examples range from the creation of the Suez Canal, the banana republics, and Fordlandia, to name a few among many.

We may also think of claims about drought being the driving force behind climate conflicts in various regions of the Arab world, Syria in particular. Such claims can serve to bolster an environmental Orientalism, in which the technologically advanced West is, once again, called upon to manage the lands for the incapable Easterners.[74] This in turn repeats the oft-cited Marxist narrative about the beginning of capitalism being the dispossession of land by military force in the name of management. So-called traditional cultures are then seen as having 'lifestyles' which can be bought and displaced without any conceptual shift or historical analysis of their structural possibilities.[75]

In a strange mutation and partial reversal of this militaristic logic of the Middle East, Reza Negarestani's *Cyclonopedia* postulates the oil reserves of the Middle East as a living entity that orchestrates the war on terror in order to liberate itself from the confines of subterranean Earth. There is an episode in the book that appears to play off the already discussed Kurtz of *Heart of Darkness* (and *Apocalypse Now*) – a rogue Delta Force soldier playing the role of Kurtz. Negarestani's book works as a counter-*Dune*: where the feudal empires of *Dune* fight over the profitable spice, in *Cyclonopedia*, oil in the Middle East, as a living entity, lures human beings so that it can be spread across the planet.

Both *Dune* and *Cyclonopedia* can be read as novels engaged with material or non-human agency. But both stories beg the question as to whether the issue is material agency or how the image of material agency is used to pivot world history. What, we should ask, are the fictional-geographical tensions in understanding such narratives in terms of small historical steps and the non-human? How, for example, are we to understand the history of a material in these contexts, or the fact that the mind-altering spice of Herbert's *Dune* was modelled after saffron (or potentially magic mushrooms)?

One still has to deal with the apparent Western humanness or alien inhumanness of the forces of capital themselves. It is thus important to ask how Negarestani's *Cyclonopedia* can be read both with and against the work of Sophia-Al Maria and Fatima Al Qadiri under the label 'Gulf Futurism'. Gulf Futurism is described as a kind of paranoid future planning, taking place despite impossible resource and geographical constraints. While Negarestani's imaginarium pulls deep on forgotten lore (albeit by puppeting popculture junk), Gulf Futurism works in part by looping and building the trashiness of 90s mall-kid video game addiction on top of hypercapitalist Gulf life. Al Qadiri's album *Desert Strike*, for instance, draws its name from a helicopter shoot-em-up game she played, in which the game's hero 'returns to the Gulf' to battle a mad dictator and protect a wealthy oil empire.[76] The thinly veiled fictions of war in the Persian gulf become far more explicit in Islamo-Futuristic texts which actively resist normalisation, such as Ahmed Saadawi's *Frankenstein in Baghdad* or Boualem Sansal's *2084*.

The ecological and the castings of Orientalism continue to travel where they have long been bound – toward war. The indistinction of war and capital (particularly after the industrial age but existing long before) paints the corporate trade wars and invasions of Indigenous lands as forms of violence which cannot be reverse engineered. But this lays down clear distinctions between human agency and environment as merely brute matter.

As one of the central perpetrators of the Bengali massacre said, as quoted by Amitav Ghosh, 'there can be no trade without war and no war without trade.'[77] Ghosh's text tells of how numerous European powers vied to control the small Banda islands, as they were the only known source of nutmeg and mace till the trees were exported by the British in the early to mid 1800s. The Dutch killed over 10,000 of the small east Indonesian islands' original inhabitants to gain control.

It is simultaneously easy and difficult to understand the justification for such slaughter for a spice. On the one hand, the justification is money, which has always been sufficient alone. But given that the object (nutmeg) seems like such a caprice, it is perhaps all the more horrifying. In such moments, it is tempting to see this capitalist violence as a kind of mad extrapolation of unhinged desire – where the market serves to depersonalise the founding acts of dispossession. But this does not explain older forms of social stratification and how these are seen to apply, or not, to those who fall outside any group's perceived borders. One can also take an ecological correlate of this where, from one group to the next, there may be a misperception about the naturalness of an environment. An example would be how European invaders in the Canadian territories saw as how 'unspoiled forest' had been, in fact, managed and terraformed for thousands of years by Indigenous peoples.

As Dian K Davis puts it, in the case of the Middle East, the "environmental imaginary" tends to view the deserts as degraded and nearing collapse, as needing to be saved from their 'reckless' Indigenous inhabitants. And alongside this, and again following Davis, one can view the properly science-fictive and misguided capitalist utopianism of the Gulf region's attempts at desalination, greening, and otherwise attempting to roll back the desert.[78]

The Middle East and Asia are both blurred by Orientalism into a technologically unstable yet alluring blankness or emptiness that justifies the unleashing of Western libido. The dreamy mirage of the East or Far East as exotic for the 'us' of the West serves to justify the 'creative' violence of desire. The Orient is an endless well of spoils or a desolated blank canvas. In both scenarios, we seem prepped for a very masculine form of desire, all the more alluring because it can be projected into a far-off cybernetic time without proper place.

Chapter 5

The Many Limbs of Empire

Science fiction's adoption and deployment of postcolonial themes is fraught with danger to both sides. On the genre's front, such adoption risks transforming the text into an allegory, with aliens becoming mere ciphers for disenfranchised Third World natives. This flattens out the cognitive aspect of sci-fi and diminishes the ethical and philosophical challenges of the figure of the alien.[79]

Elana Gomel's book *Science Fiction, Alien Encounters, and the Ethics of Posthumanism: Beyond the Golden Rule*, includes a chapter entitled 'Human Skins, Alien Masks: Allegories of Postcolonial Guilt' in which the broader theme of her book comes into focus. While posthumanism does, she argues, deal with various ontological transformations, it nonetheless upholds a humanist ethics. Gomel thus highlights the double-edged sword of posthuman uses of sci-fi; more specifically, she takes issue with science fiction and postcolonialism being used together to expand humanism (and universal 'man') rather than challenge it and its outdated ethical commitments. But as we have seen with Wynter's work in particular, decolonial thought aims towards taking apart assumptions like 'the universal human' by being critical of both humanism and of any provincial understanding of the human. Put differently, Wynter and Gomel both propose a posthumanism that is ontological and critical. To do otherwise would be to assume that science fiction, or even the themes of science fiction, only belong to the West, and this would make the very idea of futurity or universality doomed in advance.

Gomel writes:

> For postcolonialism, the representation of the human cultural Other as an ontological alien carries unintended political consequences. SF, as Langer points out, often translates cultural difference into corporeal terms. But an underlying premise of postcolonialism is the disjunction between nature and culture. Racism is wrong because we all belong to the same species and thus have the same rights. Fictional worlds in which this is not the case may create uncomfortable challenges for the ethics and politics of equality.[80]

In essence, Gomel is arguing that we have to suspend the ontological reading of science fiction in order to see the allegory that postcolonial (and decolonial) readings invite. Gomel discusses Donald A. Wollheim's short story "Mimic" (1942) (adapted as a film by Guillermo del Toro in 1997) as an example of Homi Bhabha's concept of mimicry, whereby there is an imperfect copying or blending-in of the colonised into the coloniser. The colonised is forced into imitation of an introduced, domineering alien culture, but at the same time, a potential site for subversion is opened up, which mocks or destabilises the purported difference and hierarchy between coloniser and colonised. This is where mimicry edges its way towards what Bhabha calls 'hybridity', of which Gomel gives "Lilith's Brood" by Octavia Butler, whom I discussed above, as an example.

Gomel goes on to state that,

> in discussing 'Mimic' as an allegory of cultural assimilation, we are forced to disregard its literal meaning. To describe a colonial subject as a 'bug' is to inflict a grave insult; but the creature in the tale is an

insect. In fact, the story's success depends precisely on the careful working out of the implications of biological evolution in an artificial environment.[81]

Critiquing the films *District 9* and *Mimic*, Gomel argues that there are some sci-fi texts that manage to disrupt the 'lets all get along', knee-jerk humanism of what she sees as the usual interplay between science fiction and postcolonial theory by way of allegory (though, in the end, she only offers one instance, Michael Bishop's *Transfigurations*). But the depth of the allegorical problem vis-à-vis cognitive estrangement that Gomel brings up does, I believe, indicate a different form of decoloniality.

As Gomel writes, hybridity and mimicry within a science-fiction text are redoubled because we know it is, or could be, allegorical. The hybridities and mimicries within the novel – which could be cultural, ontological, or material in various ways – can be seen as holding a relation to aspects in 'our world'. Again, following Wynter or Jackson, we should question who the 'our' or 'we' is referring to. The lingering question is, What, if anything, guarantees that the structure of allegorical relations can be read across the fictional/non-fictional divide in the way the author intends (if this even matters)? For instance, if there is a material transformation (a human becomes an alien willingly or unwillingly, with all the gray worlds to inhabit in between) what does it mean if we read this in cultural terms or technological terms (assuming we do not read it literally or even materially given that we have not yet encountered an alien body)? Butler's "Blood Child" (examined in Chapter 2) does not have the fuzzy humanism that Gomel connects to Butler's *Xenogenesis Trilogy*. Whilst it can be read in terms of the painfulness of settlement between cultures, it can also be seen to present a possible future in terms of the compromises humans would have to make in order to avoid being either coloniser or colonised.

This speculative aspect of the allegory is downplayed in Gomel's analysis in the sense of asking how we would react to novel situations in which our appeal to standard humanism cannot and should not happen. This, of course, requires seeing the allegorical connections as projective rather than primarily retrospective and reflective.

In essence, this critique of Gomel's approach to reading science-fiction stories in terms of world-making is a variation on Suvin's 'cognitive estrangement', especially in terms of temporal compression. Recall that, for Suvin, cognitive estrangement is the name for the main effect of science fiction in which the reader is dislodged from the familiar, and what is taken for granted is made strange. The idea that a story is merely an analogy or allegory can diffuse this effect and restate the division between fact and fiction.

A particular analogy or aspect of a story that indexes a far future (or a deep past) compresses it into a particular episode. A somewhat narratologically benign form of this would be the 'ancient alien' trope (in which knowledge from, or about, a long dead race is sought out). But this theme quickly expands into various speculative regimes of anthropology and coloniality: for example, in the notion of Precursors or 'ancient ones' which engineered (*Prometheus*) or seeded the cosmos with life (in Chapter 1 we saw this in terms of the Fermi Paradox) or raised only the human race for future use (*Alien vs Predator*) etc. One could even see the obsidian monoliths from Clarke's and Kubrick's *2001* as a kind of cosmological cargo cult in which the natives require technological uplift, or might worship an alien piece of technology as if it is a holy grail.

The works of H.P. Lovecraft are an early example of this 'ancient alien technology' trope, with synthetic bio-slaves running amok in the glacial wastes because their masters have long departed. The impossible architecture of Lovecraft's Great Old Ones takes on the form of colonial disbelief in works of 'alternative archaeology' like *The Chariot of the Gods*, in which aliens are put forward as the true creators of the ancient wonders of the world.

There is, then, at the other end of the spectrum from alien intervention in the lives of the ancient, a strange *a priori* disbelief in non-European empires or civilisations; a seeming prerequisite to justify the mimesis required of colonised subjects. As we have seen in Chapter 3, the colonial West seems to insist that it has been, and always will be, the model of civilisation. Evidence of technological advancement in colonised cultures thus threatens to undermine the colonists' justifications of violence (as in the case of La Casas, as we saw in the discussion of Jackson and Wynter).

The incursions of the British Empire by way of the East India Company (who we encountered already in Chapter 1) and their Dutch companions (seen in Chapter 4) are perhaps the best-known case of this. From the 1600s the Companies, along with various other European colonial ventures, established trade routes and fortresses along the coast of the subcontinent. When the company's profits were endangered, the British Crown would back them with military force. This also leads to an altogether different notion of hybdridty in terms of the colonies, use as a testing ground for techniques to be brought back home.[82]

As Suparno Banerjee has argued in his fantastic study *Indian Science Fiction*, it is obviously important to note and to explore the fact that much of the discourse on Indian science fiction focuses more on the Orientalist stereotypes than about discussing the works of Indian authors. Banerjee argues that it could be India's contact with the British Empire that may have instigated or at least accelerated such stories.[83] Science fiction in India served to explore the limits of science, speculate about feminist utopia, and even engage in nationalistic world-building, most famously seen in *Sultana's Dream* by Begum Rokeya.

We must ask, then, how to invert the problem posited by Gomel, regarding the either/or choice of literal and figurative meaning as it plays out in the notion of hybridity and mimicry. There are several examples of reversing or turning stereotypes against the means of colonisation, but this takes on an added layer of complexity when it comes to science fiction. In particular, there are instances where insect imagery is used against the forces of particularly British colonisation.[84]

Several texts have recently appeared on the entomo-politics of British–Indian relations, allowing us to consider how the political use and abuse of the notion of hybridity has become rife with biocultural traps regarding the inheritance of supposedly natural hierarchies. The caste system is itself an odd hybrid – as the word is a Portuguese imposition on two other existing forms of categorisation: *Varna* and *Jati*. The former indexes a concept of birthright while the latter is a social identity more closely connected to types of labour. The history is massively complex, so here I will focus only on how science fiction has absorbed these notions as insectoid (and how the notion of caste is bound up with insect societies).[85] The Marxist sociologist and Black radical intellectual Oliver Cox in 1945 compared the caste system to insects:

> So far as production is concerned, the caste system is not unlike, in functional conceptualization, a colony of ants or bees, with each class of insects doing its work naturally and harmoniously. Human beings may put varying estimates on the work of each class of insects; yet, for the continuance of the insect society, the work of each may be indispensable. And so, too, it is a postulate of the caste system that the occupation of the lowest caste, though relatively inferior, is nonetheless important to the system. We may take our analogy a little farther in observing that castes are supposed to work with the same

sort of symbiotic harmony as the insects, neither envying nor usurping each other's functions.[86]

This interlacing of insects and caste can and has been stretched in terms of both empire and science fiction, from the entomo-politics disrupting the bureaucratic reach of the British Empire to the science-fictive connection of caste and insectoid life in, for example, Lindsay Ellis's *Axiom's End*.[87] One can also look at the Antasy series by Clark Thomas Carlton in which the intelligent ants are divided into a caste system that has more than biological consequences.[88]

The connections of insects – ants in particular – to empire, and to the relation of instinct and reason, is of course present in broader themes within science fiction. Charlotte Sleigh's 'Empire of the Ants' highlights various connections between the portrayal of ants as the most complex instinctual menace and the power of crowds and swarms.[89] In reference to India, Sleigh quotes the first Imperial Entomologist to India, Harold Maxwell-Lefroy:

> The senses, the instincts, the modes of expression of insects are so totally diverse from our own that there is scarcely any point of contact. ... [A] locust swarm may be the product of a blind impulse ... just as a blind impulse ranges through a crowd of human beings. ... [W]ere [insects] possessed of higher forms of mentality ... no-one can say what might be the course of the world's history. ... [A] combination of the red ants could probably drive human beings out of India ... and human methods of warfare would require to be revolutionised to deal with it.[90]

While Cox's musings quoted above compare humans directly to insects, Sleigh shows how insects are used to discuss Indians as a threat to colonial power by way of actual insects. The white ants discussed by Sleigh are metaphorical stand-ins for those who would threaten the bureaucratic authority of the British in India, something emphasised in the picture of wood pulp-eating ants.

A future-oriented dystopianism can, of course, exaggerate or indenture the notion of caste. In "The Making of Pakistani Sci-Fi", Anmol Irfan[91] discusses how the short film *Shehr e Tabassum* (*City of Smiles*) sparked controversy regarding the contemporary political climate vis-à-vis the perception of an Islamic life (whatever that may mean for Westerners and others).[92] The film depicts a future state in which it is against the law not to smile, and every citizen is fixed with a device called a merry-face that seems to strangle people into smiling all the time.[93] The film emphasises the internal pressures of social roles, but here it is not those constructed by caste that are looked at but rather the inner, emotional-religious life.

City of Smiles also indexes what was discussed in Chapter 1 regarding the plurality of modernities and assumptions about technologies. The roots of science fiction (as a purportedly Western construct) often suggests a hard distinction between technology and magic, between rationality and emotionalism reflecting the naive Cartesianism we discussed in Chapter 2. Ironically, these boundaries – at their most clear in the proto-sci-fi form of the scientific romance – are decided by irrational myths and beliefs (such as the formalisms of Christian man).

One must also examine South Asian sci-fi in terms of its roots, and propose a different grounding model than the synthesis of the scientific romance and the lost-world narrative. This should be especially clear given that certain limited caricatures of the 'Far East' formed part of the stock images of lost civilisations. Indian and South Asian sci-fi needs to be articulated in a way that is not merely reactive to the incursions of British Empire, nor merely reacting against it being placed in a fixed position in the Western imaginary – namely, as an 'old world' already lost to time.

This task is further complicated by the languages of science fiction. Nudrat Kamal writes that when use of English began to equal Urdu and Bengali, this not only represented cultural encroachment but also offered a way to speak back to the history of imperialism.[94] She cites Amitav Ghosh's *Calcutta Syndrome* as one of the first instances of postcolonial South Asian science fiction. She also provides a litany of more recent examples:

> The best of South Asian SFF is that which casts in a new light our turbulent history to imagine different presents and futures. For example, Indian writer Vandana Singh's short story 'A Handful of Rice' takes place in an alternate part of South Asian history where the Mughal Empire gave way not to the British Empire, but an era of a syncretic empire with technological advances and steampunk wonders.

Sri Lankan writer Yudhanjaya Wijeratne's ongoing trilogy, *The Commonwealth Empire*, imagines the character Kandy in an alternate future in which the British Empire never fell but remained strong through advanced technology. Mary Anne Mohranraj, another Sri Lankan writer (from the diaspora), wrote a delightful novella, *The Stars Change*, set on a technologically advanced, distant planet colonised by South Asian people, which playfully explores gender, sexuality, and intimacy against the backdrop of colonialism, caste, and race.

Another particularly compelling example is Indian writer Prayaag Akbar's novel *Leila* (published in 2017, recently turned into a Netflix TV show helmed by Deepa Mehta), set in a futuristic Indian city which, due to a scarcity of water and the rise of religious authoritarianism, is segregated into sectors based on caste and religion.[95]

In addition, the question of the science of science fiction is troubled not only by the genre markers dividing or not dividing fantasy from science fiction but also by what is considered scientific – even if only by its appearance. In other words, the science of science fiction is still too often assumed to be a technological one, when in fact, much of the science of Western science fiction is less and less interested in what contemporary developments in science might mean.

For instance, Christine Hone looks at the stories and non-fiction writings of Jagadish Chandra Bose.[96]

Bose's story 'Runaway Cyclone' (written in 1896 and released in the 1920s) is read by Hone as a writing back against the legacy of British colonialism. The story lampoons the limitations of Western science to explain the behaviour of a cyclone while the Indigenous knowledge of the story's main characters is drawn upon to successfully depower the storm.

Usman T. Malik also distorts the authority of Western science, but in a somewhat different manner. His story 'The Vaporization Enthalpy of a Peculiar Pakistani Family' explores the lives of a family torn apart by violence in Pakistan. The straightforward account is somewhat oddly accompanied by oblique references to monsters interspersed with descriptions of the various phase transitions of matter (plasmas, evaporation, fusion, and so on). The issue is not so much about the explanatory power of the natural sciences; rather, it is about how the authority behind them is grounded firmly in their being Western, thereby bracketing off certain other forms of knowledge due to their provenance.

This brings us to a distinction that is massively troubling for genre purists and for passive fans of science fiction – that of fantasy from science fiction. When casually thrown together, there is an implication of similarity, at least in terms of taste, that implies a shared logic. On a shallow level, one might see them as escapist or as fantastical, in that both genres deal with the impossible – be that 'not yet' possible or 'never will be' (and 'never has been') possible. This is why so much mileage has been gotten out of Arthur C. Clarke's claim that '[a]ny sufficiently advanced technology is indistinguishable from magic.'[97] As we have seen, if the line between science fiction and fantasy is drawn from the West, then this division is going to drag other divisions with it, such as reason/emotion or human/animal. This connects to the relation, or at least view thereof, on the postcolonial and the decolonial: where the former is writing from within but against the colonial, the latter interrogates the very grounds of possibility of colonialism in order to reset all these divisions.

When looking at non-Western cultures and science fiction, the lines between the two may seem erased to Western readers or observers, since the assumption in much science fiction is that technological thinking proceeds through the elimination of the magical, or that superstitious thinking is anathema to technoscientific and hence 'rational' thinking. Even if this were true (and I do not believe it is), one would have to notice how pre- or non-scientific desires and drives motivate the shape that technology takes. Given this, science fiction can be viewed as a kind of fantasy. If there is a more recognisable difference, it may be that fantasy is often about an invented or lost past, a time when dragons or elves or myths lived and strode upon Earth. But when we shift towards the religious or deeper cultural roots of these fantasies, it becomes clear that there is concept-creep between myth and foundational ideas. Magic looks increasingly like ideas or concepts with pragmatic purchase, even if their original meaning or deepest causes are not satisfactorily known.

If the general story of disenchantment fails, then it becomes even more tempting to see science fiction as a domain of the future, of what may be. Of course, if the future is re-enchanted – or, at least, not disenchanted in a parochially Western fashion

– then there emerges the possibility of futurities not driven by the all-too-familiar technological drives. I would argue that much of Western science fiction, particular film and television, remains caught between Cyberpunk Grit or Cosmopolitan Twee. The former rehashes or remakes capitalist-realist cyberpunk nightmares (with some twists), while the latter pluralises the *Star Wars* or *Star Trek* models of intergalactic democracy.

It remains a question whether the analogous inclusiveness of past science fiction was more effective given its clandestine form, or whether more explicit identity politics performs a necessary prodding of a fanbase with latent right-wing politics. Not that these modes are mutually exclusive, but when the latter sets itself as being the end goal rather than the necessary starting ground, science fiction starts to lose its capacity for cognitive estrangement. If science fiction is merely fiction, then gaining any sense of its politics can be read as breaking the fourth wall, that is, as betraying the fictiveness of science fiction. Of course, the traces and lineages of science fiction were political from the beginning, so now the future of science fiction would seem to lead away from cognitive estrangement (in the form of casual allegory or analogy) and instead be about explicitly speaking from the point of view of other cultures.

This takes as back to where we began – to the limits of postcoloniality and how science fiction as a decolonial literature must work differently. The difference does not lie in the numerous hybridities discussed in this chapter, but rather in the rewriting of the conceptual and cultural assumptions at the very beginning of science fiction – without, of course, demolishing the possibilities of the genre itself. It lies in asking the question of what a global science fiction can be, without it being merely variations on a theme decided from a Christian cosmos.

Conclusion: Colonial Ends

The exploration of space has a long historical bond to cosmopolitan and universal projects that speak of a unified humanity or mankind. As we have repeatedly seen, this too often leads to a very white and Western 'us', or worse, it still deploys language which has its history in settler colonialism – the final frontier, space colonisation, and so on.

Deondre Smiles, in a piece entitled 'The Settler Logics of Outerspace', connects the more recent pushes towards colonising Mars (and beyond) to the tradition of treating space inhabited by Indigenous peoples as empty (*terra nullius*). As I emphasised at the beginning of this book, and have argued throughout, the question 'Is it inhabited?' appears as the central link in the science-fictive imagination and the settler (or more broadly colonial) attempts to take advantage of Indigenous peoples and their lands. While Smiles rightly highlights the troubling historical legacy of the space race – particularly its militarism and imperialism – he seems to suggest that this damns the exploration of space as such.

I feel that the possibility of a common goal or great task of leaving the planet is something worth saving but that it has to be wrested from the hands of militarists and hyper-capitalists. This common task again highlights the problem of how to talk about a 'we' – a solution is imperative not only for talking about the exploration of space but also for addressing the Anthropocene.

Contemporary theoretical discourse addressing the Anthropocene often solicits the following series of interrelated comments:

1. that the Eurocentrism of the humanities ignores that Indigenous peoples have and/or are already experiencing genocide;

2. that it is human hubris that is ultimately to blame for anthropogenic climate change (at a species level);
3. that particular organisations of social and political relations have terraformed the planet for the worse (capitalism, nationalism, etc).

In turn, each of these comments tends towards a particular formulation of the figure of the human or the 'we':

1. critiques the rational Western subject and has received a number of articulations in post- and decolonial approaches;
2. emphasises a non-human agency at the base of – and in relation to / conflict with – human capacity;
3. draws responses from critical or genealogical humanism and post-humanisms (Marx/Freud/Foucault) that attack the historically dominant forms of knowledge in the political-social domain.

Given the temporal nature of the Anthropocene (as a geological age), the subject of extinction raises two related problems: first, the contrasting temporal and spatial dimensions of extinction (what does it mean to say extinction is already occurring and has yet has to occur?); and, secondly, the continuity between humans and non-human animals. These are obviously entwined because the question of whether extinction affects only specific biological categories or, rather, all groups of living things touches upon issues of how animal-like humans are. Whereas the continuity between humans and animals manifests itself negatively in de- and postcolonial critiques (which deal firstly with the making of some humans into beasts by others) of some humans, it can also function in a constructive way by indexing Indigenous cosmologies which actively erode the comfortable distinctions between human and animal.

Likewise, non-human approaches make supposed human differences a result of lower-level material agency, which arguably broadens the notion of the political but at the potential cost of human histories and problems (which undermines the genealogical approach of assuming at least a formal stability to the human).

The question of 'an end' in these different trajectories of interpreting the Anthropocene goes beyond extinction. In addition to the questions about who constitutes 'we' (and who decides) the discourse on extinction suggests a framework which relies upon different terms or on a different matrix of interpretation: culture-people-genocide; civilisation-world-apocalypse; and, finally, planet-life-extinction. Hopefully, the correspondences of the triads above are clear: decoloniality emerges from the persistent logic of culture-people-genocide; technological and active materiality addresses civilisation-world-apocalypse; while the dominant forms of history and scientific knowledge seem to lay claim to planet-life-extinction.

There is, of course, drift and contestation within and across each domain. In this conslusion, I will engage with the work of Wynter, Tallbear, Todd, Whyte, Danowski, Viveiros de Castro, and others to discern the critical differences between the various ends of the world (or worlds) – in genocides, apocalypses, and extinctions – in order to see the limits of Anthropocene discourse and how this can inform understanding in the historical sciences. More specifically, I will look at how biological thinking, which is central to thinking extinction, has been perpetually pushed away from being a historical science (which generally includes geology, palaeontology, archaeology, cosmology, etc). Unearthing biology's status as a historical science is one means of making possible even small steps towards decolonising biology and the philosophy of biology.

There has been an explosion of work which attempts to shift the beginnings of the Anthropocene or to otherwise restructure the narrative by tracing its relation to the legacy of colonialisation. This highlights not only the extractive aspects of the various stages of colonialism (Dutch, Spanish, British, North American, and so on) but also the redistribution of resources and territory and the extermination of peoples for the sake of feeding empire. These horrors are too often relegated to the past as from the time of colonialism (whatever that should actually mean) as different from neo-colonialism. The question persists as to whether 'neo-colonialism' is a term applied only to those who did not perpetuate it in previous iterations but now do, albeit in so-called 'softer forms' – Brazil and China in particular.

In the cause of genocide by other cultural formations, the shadow term is of course that of people where what counts as human functioned as an exposed network that was largely religious (or we might say theological) in principle. This capacity and formulation of the human corresponds to Sylvia Wynter's Man1: namely, the conception of humans as rational-political beings corresponding to its formulation by the West from the Renaissance to the eighteenth century. She calls this (with particular reference to the Spanish invasion of the Americas) the creation of *Homo politicus*.

It is then in the eighteenth century that this theological-humanist model gives way – slowly, in fits and starts – to an economical-biological model. But even with the historical shift away from the ancient and medieval orders to a one-of-a-kind theological-subject, the tensions between reason and piety in the actions of the conquistadors emerge as claims about reading cultural practices into the constitution of people. As Wynter puts it,

> The quite Other form of life and mode of being human of the indigenous peoples were therefore simply seen by the

Spaniards as the irrational Lack of their own. So that even when confronted, as in the case of the Aztecs, with the latter's complex and well-organized imperial civilization – one, however, based on the central institution of large-scale human sacrifice – Sepúlveda was able to argue that this practice by itself was clear evidence of the Aztecs' lack of 'natural reason': of their having therefore been determined by 'natural law' to be the 'natural slaves' of the Spaniards.[98]

For the clergy, Wynter explains, these practices were rational relative to the community standards of the Indigenous population (the logic of sacrifice as such is rational to any given social political form), but this does not make it any less impious. Of course, this is not to say that the Christian (or any religious) mode of ranking is less disastrous than a secular one, but the work that is done to make them conciliatory (or not) exposes the implicit definitional violence of this or that ordering of the world.

In terms of the discourses on race leading up to the formation and naming of biology in the early 1800s – conducted by numerous figures at once – it was the voices of theologists that asserted the unity of the human race (as all descendants of Adam and Eve), while freethinkers like Voltaire would insist that the 'races of man' were different species.

This is not to repeat the general reproach that categorisation is only ever a means of domination; rather, it is to suggest that categorisation has dominatory affects – intentionally or not – especially when it becomes or is presented as historical. For all of Linneaus's categories, the fact that he puts humans within the system of nature (however wrongly championed as its pinnacle) pushed against prevailing human exceptionalism. Whilst the formal subject may borrow from the theological model, the two are not collapsed together, and the possibility remains that a formal or abstract notion of the subject can sidestep a discourse that has become dominant in an ahistorical or provincial form. To put this more directly, how do we decide what sets humans apart from animals without falling into Christian theological traps about human (read Western) superiority?

Fanon, whom Wynter discusses at length, utilised Hegelian concepts of the struggle to consciousness against the immediate conditions of his life, as well as against the Eurocentric conceptions of that Hegelian identity (something we discussed in Chapter 2). Again, while not theological, the universal or abstract forms of subjectivity (in terms of the meaning of self, or desire, or consciousness) may also be too stuck in their European cradle. This conundrum is what Wynter calls Man1.

Wynter then discusses the shift to Man2, to a bio-centric definition following Darwin's contribution to the biological sciences. She writes:

> This principle, that of bio-evolutionary Natural Selection, was now to function at the level of the new bourgeois social order as a de facto new Argument-from-Design – one in which while one's selected or dysselected status could not be known in advance, it would come to be verified by one's (or one's group's) success or failure in life.[99]

For Wynter, the concepts swirling around the industrial revolution led to a mutation of what constituted the generic human, from the perspective of the powerful within Europe. Rather than a special status guaranteed by Christian cosmology, the human now became defined by a social-Darwinist code of the strongest or the fittest. This was far more compatible with the accelerating expansionist and capitalist logic riding the second wave of colonialism.

Against Foucault, Wynter argues that there is, in fact, a continuous construction of the human that underlies the supposed episteme shifts within the sciences concerning the image of the human. Wynter argues that the underlying grand narrative of Judaeo-Christian humanity persists, albeit transformed, through the historical shifts because these all occur within a particular Western frame.

Histories and philosophies of biology similarly take issue with Foucault's model of changing epistemes or paradigms as particularly ill-fitting to biology. The massive complication with Wynter's account of Darwin is in part due to the fact that she implicitly combines a discussion of *On the Origin of Species* and *The Descent of Man* and names only Darwin in perpetuating a bourgeois social order built upon biocentrism. But it could be argued that the persistence of the construct of Man1 (the human as a Christian being) that was reapplied to Darwin's theory by explicitly rejecting natural selection because of its denial of human purposiveness. Few figures accepted the radical contingency that natural selection required and could not accept it for decades. The racism of *The Descent of Man* is largely the result of Darwin's redeploying the discourse of progress into one of development, though his interest, as Wynter highlights, is more about pressing the notion of common origin and reducing the gaps between animals and humans.

The maintenance of a hierarchy of control post-Darwin becomes far more subtle, and its paradoxical formation is what makes possible the devaluation of peoples and cultures by way of scientific racism. As Jessica Riskin has brilliantly pointed out, the neo-Darwinian paradigm denies the contingency of natural selection to the extent that life can be a controlled mechanism, and it is this view that feeds most directly into a crypto-progressiveness.

Thus, the retroactive formulation of genocide as a concept in the closing days of WWII is articulated in relation to the technological possibility of death, but when projected into the past, the articulation of peoples relative to dehumanisation becomes more apparent. For instance, when the biologist and historian of biology Ernst Mayr writes that the history of human beings is a history of genocide, he is applying the term between species of *Homo*. If this were, in fact, the case, it would be a war between species of a genus, and not a war of one species. But this would bracket out the relation to non-human species – both companion species as well as those hunted or raised. There is then, in fact, a perverse atavism – a retro move – in the introducing of races (later softened by UNESCO decree into 'ethnic groups after the holocaust'), which essentially attempts to reintegrate the pre-history of prehistory into the history of human beings – for example, in the form of germs or dispositions or tendencies. Even proponents of monogenism, such as Kant, had to explain why there were five races and not four.

As we have seen, the problem is also explored in the work of Kimberly Tallbear, who notes the political uses of blood quantum, whereby governmental recognition of belonging to am Indigenous American tribe (or not) is established by tracing lineage. She counters that,

> regarding the issue of Native American identity, the main problem is not the fact that the genetic technology cannot reveal all lines of biological descent. Even if advances in genetic science, or the use of additional genetic tests for additional markers, were to enable greater certainty in determining a person's descent from 'Native American' ancestors, the act of using science in that way is a technological manifestation of sociopolitical ideas of race. Such ideas assert that cultural identity can be conclusively established in an individual's biology. Science cannot prove an individual's identity as a member of a cultural entity such as a tribe; it can only reveal one individual's genetic inheritance or partial inheritance. The two are not synonymous.[100]

The question raised by genocide is that there would seem to be an imperative to recognise the contingency of evolution, in that there is one species, and divisions within that species are not biological differences but scientifically racist accounts of biological concepts (often freighted with non-biological Judaeo-Christian schema). These latter are used to 'naturalise' the actions of one people over and against another in the name of recognising diversity or plurality.

Wynter and Tallbear demonstrate how the neo-Darwinian paradigm in biology leads to a techno-scientific politics. This refuses to question the status quo which is built upon and eagerly attempts to extend a colonial history, both forwards and backwards in time. The only addition or extension I would hope to make (given my position and my knowledge) is that biology as a wider discourse should not be surrendered to contemporary neo-Darwinians such as Richard Dawkins and Stephen Pinker. There is an alliance between purposive anthropology and mechanistic functionalism that allows for descriptive jumps between individual and culture, yet in which the whole middle ground of historical and material change is neglected. Take, for example, this claim from Pinker:

> In short, the existence of environmental mitigations doesn't make the effects of the genes inconsequential. On the contrary, the genes specify what kinds of environmental manipulations will have what kinds of effects and with what costs. This is true at every level, from the expression of the genes themselves ... to large-scale attempts at social change. The totalitarian Marxist states of the twentieth century often succeeded at modifying behaviour, but at the cost of massive coercion, owing in part to mistaken assumptions about how easily human motives would respond to changed circumstances.[101]

Here, as throughout the whole essay from which it is pulled, Pinker attempts to establish guilt by association (environmentally focussed people are totalitarians) and claims that a position closer to genetic determinism would be more rational and more amenable to the West.

Pinker's position can be described as a response to what Amia Srinivasan has called response to 'genealogical anxiety': even though there is no reason why we have arrived at this point, since we are here we can make our own luck and become lords of the cultural domain built on top of the evolutionary one. The mechanical function coupled with the progressivist re-articulation means that we are capable of technically directing this progression into the future. But this genealogy, again following Srinivasan, is about whether we are justified in what we believe, and it is less concerned with what is important for the posthumanism mentioned at the beginning. Put another way, it does not ask what our beliefs do because of their history.[102]

The technological extension of the human's biological basis grounds but does not adequately articulate the normative or narrativist aspect of the human as historical being. If we read these splits backwards, as it were – for example, seeing the formation of peoples as above speciation – they clearly play as big of a role in genocidal thought as does its technological expression (based upon geographical location and resource use). Furthermore, while the continuity between humans and animals serves extinction thinking, it does not serve cultural thought in terms of peoples as divisions within one category. In cultural narratives of a people's existence, such distinctions are historical rather than a difference within the existing continuity of all life.

But before discussing that aspect, I will first look at the most prevalent form of human extinction in fiction, that of the Civilisation-World-Apocalypse cluster. Civilisation is generally thought to be a progressive development of a cultural form such that there are both social and technological high-order structures. Civilisation (or civilisations) is of course overwhelmingly a product of Western history, and is dominated by narratives of rise and fall (especially of empires), such as in the work of Oswald Spengler. Often, here, civilisation encompasses a generic notion of 'the world', but the term can and has been put forward as a comparative unit to de-colonialise what counts as 'advanced', for example relative to urban consolidation, agricultural development, community organisation, and so forth. Post-apocalyptic fantasies which talk about the end of the world generally mean the 'civilised world' or civilisation, but not the destruction of the planet or the immediate end of the human race (or species).

The coupling of civilisation and apocalypse in science fiction (the death of all life by other lifeforms) is often technologically mediated, for example in dating the 'golden spike' of the Anthropocene to the first detonations of nuclear weapons (hence 'nuclear apocalypse' or 'nuclear Armageddon') – or, in a similar way, dating it, as Paul J. Crutzen does, to the invention of the steam engine in the 1740s. Just as the Anthropocene has technological capacity at its centre, the question becomes, How central are these capacities to how we define the human in a global sense?

Dipesh Chakrabarty's essay "'The Climate of History" is often invoked in a call for a unified 'we' or an 'us' that must face the global crises of anthropogenic climate change; it is a task, he argues, that requires the deployment of a historical category of human or the human species. His approach to the conceptual core of a shared notion of human species rests on the possibility of a negative universal history – a human history that constructs itself against the crimes of attempts to 'civilise the world', and finds a hope in commonality due to our shared existential threat (cultural particulars are collected but not subsumed, contra Hegel).

Deborah Danowski and Eduardo Viveiros de Castro in *The Ends of the World* argue that Chakrabarty overlooks ethnographic theories which could contribute to a shared generic subject of a negative universal history. Rather than prioritising species being, they argue, this would position the human as a generator of myths and of ways of being, and thus recognise this universal characteristic of humankind (of having a way of being) as also present in non-human species. Danowski and Viveiros de Castro contrast Chakrabarty's approach with that of the post-war phenomenologist and philosopher of technology Gunther Anders, who suggested we entertain stories and fantasies of the end of the world so as to avoid it – citing as an example nuclear Armageddon, but also aware that he was writing in the wake of the Holocaust.

The fact that the end of the world does not mean the end of the planet necessarily implies attempts to restart 'civilisation', and highlights the founding acts of violence and the kind of libertarian fantasies (present in zombie apocalypses in particular) where the office worker can now be a great warrior, the suburbanite becomes a DIY specialist, and so forth.

Andreas Malm and Alf Hornborg rally against numerous attempts to see a singular technological cause of the Anthropocene and staunchly believe that it is only the organisation of human socio-political relations. Following Marx against Chakrabarty, Malm and Horborg apparently do not recognize that Chakrabarty is following the early Marx in terms of the notion of species being – humans as the animals which change themselves. There is, here, a different claim about the scope of history and humans as prehistorical in social terms or technological terms (where the latter tends to be told in individualistic ways).

If the first cluster discussed (Culture-People-Genocide) was retroactive in its combination of anthropology and biology, then the question of 'worlds' sees a recombination of threats relative to the perceived stability of the modern. One (often a white man)

Conclusion: Colonial Ends

fantasises about going back to how things were or establishing a new, better, 'simpler' world. Here, the apocalyptic is subtractive as a genre, as it selectively removes elements of 'the world' to construct the wasteland that remains. The genre allows for the past world to be 'erased' as the world-builder desires while giving the world-builder the freedom to mythologise those past relics either wholly or partially buried in time. This can be seen in works as different as NK Jemisin's *Broken Earth* trilogy to Mande's *Station Eleven*.

The genre is thus past-directed, but in a way that builds a near-future from a freely recombined past. The very form of post-apocalyptic tales denies any imagination of a future that is not an elaborate junkyard of the past and near-future. An emblematic figure of this is 'the man and dog', which indexes the fantasies of a new tribe, and the beginning of civilisation as domestication (as well as indexing the human-animal continuity so important to the discourse on extinction). But this we will address below.

These fantasies of domestication are telling with regard to our communal self-reflections on the current relationship between politics and technology. The combined effect of the (often) technological cause and the selective erasure of the present-as-past is that the present is inevitability doomed, yet elements can be selectively resurrected. This allows an odd combination of preparatory eschatology and a total removal from the political or environmental present.

While the post-apocalyptic frame allows for potentially revolutionary experiments in genre recombination, it often exhibits conservative microcosms of social and political fantasies. The genre exposes the basic sociopolitical fantasies of the West, regarding the question of whether humans are animals that require control or whether, rather, control turns humans into animals. By referring to the particularities of the present, post-apocalyptic fictions serve to entertain left-

and right-wing fantasies about escaping contemporary life in their relative forms – both the conservative desire to start over in order to keep things simple or traditional and a prevalent leftist fantasy of escaping the contemporary technologically mediated world and going 'back to nature' or some other form of 'authentic' existence. Or, put otherwise, post-apocalyptica indirectly closes the ideological gap between eschatological Christian doomsayers and anarcho-primitivist radicals.

Because the structure of worlds is largely narratological (whether myths or stories), the end (beyond mass death) means a loss of meaningful structure (of law and order) or of a cosmology. This, in turn, again brings up the question of Western categorisations of knowledge and ontology. Zoe Todd's work, which comes from a stance of non-Western feminism (in all its varied forms), points out how despite Bruno Latour's cosmopolitics and invocation of thinking the planet through non-Western or non-modern thought, he remains firmly fixed within the Western canon. In this way, her critique brings together the question of multiple modernities (seen in Chapter 1) with questions around decolonial and postcolonial approaches (Chapter 4). In a similar vein to Todd, Breny Mendoza argues in her essay "'Can the subaltern save us?'" that Indigenous thought has become a myth for thought in general in the humanities – made to testify to the existence of a world before 'us' (us being technological or at least industrial humans).

As Kyle Whyte observes in '"Indigenous Science (Fiction) for the Anthropocene: Ancestral Dystopias and Fantasies of Climate Change Crises"', corroborating ideas looked at previously in this book, there are split temporalities revealed by the fact that "the hardships many non-Indigenous people dread most of the climate crisis are ones that Indigenous peoples have endured already due to different forms of colonialism: ecosystem collapse, species loss, economic crash, drastic relocation, and cultural disintegration."[103]

Whyte emphasises an important difference regarding the circuits of meaning already outlined. While extinction refers to a wide scale of life – to whole species – the articulation of collapsing apocalypse and extinction (seen from the perspective of European knowledges) would make the close relation of non-human species and the human something of the past – with these relations only be re-revealed because of ecological dependencies being disrupted. But this, of course, ignores the different formations of human and non-human relations outside the articulation of species.

Furthermore, Whyte criticises the work of allies (this would potentially include me, here and now) who place Indigenous ways of living inside a Western articulation of deep time (i.e. the holocene) as well as a particular form of articulating temporality in the sense of not only a linearity versus non-linearity but a disavowal of the ancestrality of concepts of Western thought. It is not even a question of opposing sciences to non-sciences, or Western epistemologies to non-Western epistemologies, but a question of seeing the historical nature of one's concepts relative to the aims and goals of one's epistemological programs.

This indexes Wynter's series of Man1 and Man2 (iterations of political and rational humans) as being fundamentally European myths. We could even say, again echoing Wynter's critique of Foucault, that just as the transformation of 'man' happened within a certain Western matrix, the myth discourse of even those critical of technological rationality (such as Adorno and Horkheimer) make a myth of myth, especially in the form of disenchantment. Such concepts rely upon the human as a bearer of a type of being. While this can have a formal articulation – one that attempts to be genuinely abstract – in the late nineteenth and early twentieth centuries it tended to be overtly freighted with historical cultural baggage. Typically, it did not adequately challenge the limited choices of that history, nor did it properly historicise the use of the abstract or the formal; rather, what it presented as formal or abstract was, in fact, something far more Eurocentric.

For instance, what do we make of Heidegger's or Nietzsche's seeing Greek culture as the be-all and end-all of culture as such – that is, the idea that cultural concepts and a culture that is necessarily locked into a particular place could ever be taken as universal? The question thus arises as to what limits historical context can establish faced with a limited concept knowingly universalised in the name of domination?.

This is arguably a juncture where one can demonstrate constructive possibilities for the fundamental continuity between human and animal and can, indeed, shift from the project of posthumanism (or maybe a critical posthumanism as seen in Chapter 2) to one of thinking extinction in terms of the non-human or inhuman. It is important to note, of course, that recognising a continuity between animals and humans does not stop a hierarchy being laid onto it, nor does it erase the long racist and eugenical history of comparisons to animals. This latter point is troublingly persistent (to put it mildly) in contemporary utilitarian ethics, and has been seen in Alice Crary's convincing critiques of Peter Singer.[104]

The issue is not only these comparisons; it is also the very possibility of a metric of comparison. For Singer, for instance, one might observe the material conditions and capacities of animals and disabled humans and find cause to compare their degrees of suffering. For others, the question of comparison should function at the level of affect, of emotional resonance or, in a mode more sympathetic to Crary, we might say it is a more formal matter of formal deciding what we, as humans, have to collectively determine to be ethical.

This is not to say we must reject any material considerations in looking at animals and humans. But by looking at different sensory capacities, we could emphasise moral standing as necessary, given an incommensurability between worlds – be it the ultraviolet world of a bee or the sonic world of a bat, and the more familiar visual world of humans requires that we have ethical considerations to cover over the gaps.

As we saw in Chapter 2, Jackson discusses the tendency within Animal Studies (naming Singer in particular) to deepen a generic sense of the human as it is within classical liberalism (which in turn echoes N. Katherine Hayles's concerns about the posthuman being still too human). The issue becomes one of disentangling rational ethics from the kind of value-neutral view of the world, posited by figures such as Singer. In numerous texts, Jackson has tied these concerns to animal-human relations and the discourse on race to argue that there is no conceptual world in a singular sense. Once again, we see how the previous discussion about material or formal moral standing touches upon our earlier discussions, at several points, about plural modernities and plural worlds.

We could synthesise the above in the following question: At what level does the gap between species worlds (what we can perceive) map onto different cosmologies (what human beliefs and concepts make of the world), and how does this play out in different histories (the plurality of modernities addressed at several points in this text)? Or: What modes of comparisons across worlds and times will allow 'us' to avoid falling into political and ethical traps? Following Whyte's critique, one mistake is to sympathise (from an already morally closed position) with generalised Indigenous attitudes towards non-human animals, as if this is only an ancient tradition and not a lived and pragmatic engagement. This is all too evident in the slide in language from traditional to Indigenous in terms of what is considered knowledge by white 'sympathisers'.

These relations return us back to Wynter's worries about biocentrism (via the social Darwinist construction of Man2, mentioned above), as well as Bear's concerns about biocolonialism. These worries demonstrate the complexity of posthuman and inhuman (in the case of formal articulations of thought or personhood) approaches in the wake of a humanism that was never about the human in either a biological or historical sense.

It has become almost a banal talking point that we (whatever that means in terms of the normative bounds of the human) are currently experiencing the sixth mass extinction event in Earth's known history. It is this scale of death and of the disappearance of species that dominates the concept of extinction. The K-Pg (Cretaceous–Paleogene) extinction of the dinosaurs was possibly the most dramatic, given the suddenness and extent of the asteroid impact, but earlier extinctions were even more deadly in terms of the forms of life destroyed (the great dying of the P-T or Permian Triassic Extinction for example).

The temporally extended nature of planetary extinction and its purported externality as a sudden event make understanding the current ongoing mass extinction difficult to see (as extinction would be seen as coming from without). Put otherwise, extinction is harder to think when it is neither a catastrophic event nor one that happened long ago; extinction seems to rest uneasily in how we perceive our own human history.

When thought in human time, extinction gets converted, unwittingly or not, into apocalypse and post-apocalypse narratives. This slide happens particularly easily in terms of aesthetics – post-apocalyptic landscapes can borrow from or exploit present day imagery of ecological disaster and massive species death. Furthermore, if humans are normatively defined – again, this is overwhelmingly in the white Christian terms that 'we' are human because 'we' are cultural, 'we' are human to the extent that 'we' are 'more than' animals – then modern humans may seem external to extinction.

In *X-Risk*, Thomas Moynihan calls extinction and apocalypse false friends. He explains that, while the latter is a sense of an ending, extinction is the end of sense, an end of a way of experiencing the world. We might not ever know 'what it is like to be a bat', but we can understand that a way of knowing is lost when an ancient embodiment of it is destroyed; put another way, we know when a form of the end of sense has occurred. Or, again, a species world can be destroyed without the earth being destroyed.

It is integral for thinking extinction that we convert thinking about extinction (as the end of sense) into human terms without converting it into an apocalyptic aesthetic, and without privileging certain human views of the world (again, of there being a singular world or modernity). This involves confronting not only how the humanities think extinction but also the limits on humanity's understanding of animal life. It does not seem a stretch to say that those peoples who have been under threat of apocalypse might have an altogether different view of the possibilities of extinction.

In her conclusion to *Native American DNA*, Tallbear writes,

> I also seek out scientists who strive to bring diverse people into their fields, including indigenous scientists, but not just to cast a rainbow across the laboratory. I seek scientific coconspirators who don't think they have the gospel truth but who want to challenge the social and ethical norms of their fields not only in order to make them more inclusive but also to make the science more robust, more strongly objective.[105]

The sense that objectivity creates collectively robust and well-aligned fields across the humanities and sciences is especially strong in feminist science and technology studies, and it is especially important for biology. While Science and Technology Studies is often seen as stretched between history, sociology, and anthropology, it is, I would argue, the closest body of work to a philosophy of science in the continental tradition (following the broadly French tradition of the mid-twentieth century, which grounded thinkers such as Foucault). The question of extinction – whether applied to the human species or to all species at once (omnicide) – relies heavily upon the status of historical sciences and on their push to dehistoricise biology. Everything has a history, and every biological entity is the result of contingent constraints and material conditions that could have been otherwise.

Such dehistoricisation can be understood in three interrelated senses – the dominance of Western biology over the field in general; the lack of history within biological texts and practices; and the push to make biology an experimental science first and foremost at the cost of its historical aspects. All these aspects infect one another and provide an image of biology that lends itself to what Wynter critiques as biocentrism and what Tallbear calls biocolonialism. The growth of biological thought in the West is yoked to collections and theories precipitated by colonial pillaging and the overlay of Western aesthetic conditions upon the discourse of race (even by the more 'progressive' polygeneists such as Blumenbach). People from non-Western places were seen as not the children of Adam and Eve, as less evolved, as newer, younger, and in need of 'education'. Even when environmental conditions affected organismal development (human or otherwise), it was still something ranked, with white Europeans at the top.

This tendency was, however, challenged and disrupted – although by no means completely – by pushes in the early 1800s towards biological entities as self-organising and a generalisation of the capacities of life in the early 1800s. The organism and the living became something resistant to Cartesian thought and to easy classification. It became possible for life to have a history and for a science of it to develop that was not subordinate to other sciences.

However, the more functionalist and mechanical modes of biological interpretation took precedent in the decades preceding and immediately following Darwin. Attempts to understand inheritance of traits as well as variance across species led to statistical and formal articulations of evolution in order to bracket out degrees of unwanted complexity. A certain narrowness of focus made it possible to re-situate such technics in the name of anthropological and aesthetic biases – reinjecting teleology or purpose into biology in terms of potentials for control of the statistical frequencies and distributions of populations (rising to an exceptionally sick apogee in eugenics of the late 1800s and early 1900s).

These themes are omnipresent in 20th century science fiction and are endorsed or fought against in the earliest works of science fiction.

Whilst the legacy of eugenics has been much commented on in theoretical texts and histories of biology, this does not mean much if it is largely – almost completely – absent from biology and genetics textbooks. Moreover, the history of the period between Darwin and the Modern Synthesis of the 1920s and 1930s is ill-explored: it is sometimes portrayed as a period of dormancy (as 'the eclipse of Darwin' in Julian Huxley's famous phrase), but this is just a back-projection made from the perceived stable certainties of the age of molecular biology. The decades following the publication of *On the Origin of Species* were not a series of wrong turns, rather there was an emphasis on animal agency, on the biological roots of cognition, on the cell and its properties, and so on. A central tenet of the Modern Synthesis concerns the statistical treatment of evolution, something foregrounded for reasons very much outside the purview of biology itself.

Evolutionary and Developmental Biology (Evo-Devo for short) has put significant pressure on two important areas: namely, genetic determinism, and the concept of species as either a taxonomic formalism (traditionally established) or a population which can interbreed (swap genes). More and more, cladistics – the notion of common ancestry as a way to understand species – has come to dominate, and the approach has proven far more amenable to ecological understanding, as it can be overlaid on biography as well as morphology. This is simply to say that the history of ways of parsing species is itself increasingly lost to time (tracked imperfectly by molecular clocks and morphological comparisons). Even the question of what makes a species a species is decided by the timescale and the methods so that any act of dividing life into species risks falling foul of the impossibility of any kind of ideological neutrality.

This may all seem like too much of a digression into biology and its troubled history. But there is a deeply important conceptual aspect of Wynter's work that is, I think, important for understanding science fiction's potential relation to decoloniality. In one of her more controversial essays, entitled 'Beyond Miranda's Meanings', Wynter critiques certain (largely white) feminist analyses for being too quick to analogise certain figures in William Shakespeare's *The Tempest*. If the play symbolises the change from magic and royalty to modern statehood (where the powerful Prospero becomes more powerful when he renounces his magic and excels at political manipulation), then the other characters are different victims of this transition: Miranda stands in for dominated women, Sycorax the witch as powerful (Indigenous) femininity, Caliban for the racially oppressed, and Ariel for the indentured or indebted.

While there is a long tradition of Caliban becoming a figure for both Caribbean and some African uprisings – including Octave Mannoni's *Prospero and Caliban: The Psychology of Colonization* (1964), critique by Frantz Fanon, Aimé Césaire's *A Tempest* (1969), Kamau Brathwaite's *Barabajan Poems, 1492–*

1992, and Paget Henry's *Caliban's Reason* – these texts have been viewed as overly masculinist or focused on the violent capacity of Caliban, potentially ignoring his advances against Miranda. As Wynter points out, much feminist discourse has fought for more recognition of Miranda (despite her cruelties towards Caliban) or, more enticingly, for Caliban's mother, the powerful witch Sycorax, who is already dead by the tale's start.

But Wynter's essay makes a deeply interesting suggestion – what about Caliban's missing mate?

This is not an issue of heteronormative reproducibility but whether Caliban gets to count as even biologically human at the most basic level. Caliban is a people of one and hence not a member of the human race nor only racially coded – he seems built for extinction. It is this biological impossibility that, for Wynter, makes this absence even more interesting than Sycorax's partial absence from the play.

Wynter writes:

> Nowhere in this mutational shift from the primacy of the anatomical model of sexual difference as the referential model of mimetic ordering, to that of the physiognomic model of racial/cultural difference, more powerfully enacted than in Shakespeare's play *The Tempest*, one of the foundational endowing texts both of Western Europe's dazzling rise to global hegemony, and, at the level of human 'life', in general, of the mutation from primarily religiously defined modes of human being to the first, partly secularizing ones.[106]

Wynter's reading can also be applied to a science-fiction film adaptation of *The Tempest*, namely, *Forbidden Planet* (1956). In the film, a spaceship crew lands on a planet and finds all the inhabitants dead save a professor, his daughter, and his faithful robotic servant (correlating to Prospero, Miranda, and Ariel).

There is also a monster stalking the planet, one that is invisible until attacked. But importantly, this monster is not Caliban. The monster is the projection (by way of alien technology) of the id of Morbius, the film's Prospero. Through a science-fictive element, the film is able to make explicit the fact that Caliban is an impossible projection of Western racism, caught in the shift from a Christian self-perception to a biological-economic one. Or, put another way, we are shown the impossibility that there could exist a biological being that is fully separate from the 'we' or 'us' that build such biological categories. *Forbidden Planet*, read with Wynter's model of genealogy, shows how the scientific romance and the lost-civilisation fantasies of science fiction collapse in on themselves if the aporias of Western self-perception are not seen for all their false magnifications in the past, present, and imagined futures.

The point here is to return to what we have stated more than once about the difference between the postcolonial and the decolonial – where the latter has to be about reworking the deep conceptual commitments and the very genealogy of what made texts and narratives possible. This differs from reading a text through the lens of postcolonial critique, in that the latter can only treat this or that narrative as an example of a set worldview to be combatted, or attempt to read a text against itself (for example, by attempting to show how the colonial imaginary within a sci-fi novel is unstable, contradictory, and so on).

I have argued that the decolonial move, particularly in Wynter's work, is the far more fruitful approach when it comes to science fiction. Reading science fiction in this way makes of it a material for understanding coloniality, rather than something that is merely poisoned by it or revisable once one has sufficient knowledge of the history of empire and the history of science fiction. Reading *Forbidden Planet* through what we know about Caliban is one example of this: it is not a revisionary interpretation, nor does it suggest we abandon the film. Rather, it electrifies the entire text: the film is not deflated by applying Wynter's genealogical critique; it becomes even more worldly (something particularly important for science fiction).

The figure of Caliban can also be worked with another way, by moving to the beginning (or, at least, one possible beginning) of science fiction, namely, Mary Shelley's *Frankenstein*. As Rei Terada has shown, Caliban can and has been read as embodying the figure of the freed slave – of the human, but not-quite-human, figure who hopes to continue his own race but who, like Caliban, is denied a mate by his master. Just as Caliban is the projection of the Enlightenment attempting to move 'beyond race' and cast aside magic for statecraft, so, too, is Frankenstein's monster a reflection of Promethean hubris.

Importantly, for Caliban, as for Frankenstein's creature, this hubris must be understood to run far deeper than the merely technological; it is scientific, but also cultural and conceptual. The fact that *The Tempest* and *Frankenstein* are so bound up with Milton's *Paradise Lost* (as stories of fall and redemption by way of creation) shows how thoroughgoing Wynter's point is about the maintaining of superiority from Man1 (Christian Europe) to Man 2 (Darwinistic and Economic). Percy Shelley's preface to Mary Shelley's *Frankenstein* makes a point of saying that Darwinian theory makes *Frankenstein* possible in the same way that *Paradise Lost* makes it possible:

> The event on which this fiction is founded has been supposed, by Dr. Darwin, and some of the physiological writers of Germany, as not of impossible occurrence. I shall not be supposed as according the remotest degree of serious faith to such an imagination; yet, in assuming it as the basis of a work of fancy, I have not considered myself as merely weaving a series of supernatural terrors. The event on which the interest of the story depends is exempt from the disadvantages of a mere tale

of spectres or enchantment. It was recommended by the novelty of the situations which it develops; and, however impossible as a physical fact, affords a point of view to the imagination of the delineating of human passions more comprehensive and commanding than any which the ordinary relations of existing events can yield.

I have thus endeavoured to preserve the truth of the elementary principles of human nature, while I have not scrupled to innovate upon their combinations. The *Iliad*, the tragic poetry of Greece – Shakespeare, in *The Tempest* and *Midsummer Night's Dream* – and most especially, Milton, in *Paradise Lost*, conform to this rule; and the most humble novelist, who seeks to confer or receive amusement from his labours, may, without presumption, apply to prose fiction a licence, or rather a rule, from the adoption of which many exquisite combinations of human feeling have resulted in the highest specimens of poetry.[107]

The trajectory of Frankenstein, then, made more evident in its connections to *The Tempest*, is not about a technological Prometheus; it is about the definition of the human. This is the ground and possibility for all science fiction which *Frankenstein* popularised if not inaugurated – namely, that doing science fiction, not fantasy, means extrapolating from the world as it seems to be.[108] But, as we have seen throughout this book, the erasure of myth (or of fantasy) is the greatest myth. The founding, but also limiting, myth of science fiction is that we know what the human is and can thus analogise its limitations and – in turn – the possibilities of other forms of life. Science fiction exaggerates all the ugliness and utopian wishes of the past in equal measure. The dangers of ignoring this within ourselves were laid out by Aimé Césaire, and I give him the last word:

colonial enterprise is to the modern world what Roman imperialism was to the ancient world: the prelude to Disaster and the forerunner of Catastrophe. Come, now! The Indians massacred, the Moslem world drained of itself, the Chinese world defiled and perverted for a good century; the Negro world disqualified; mighty voices stilled forever; homes scattered to the wind; all this wreckage, all this waste, humanity reduced to a monologue, and you think all that does not have its price? The truth is that this policy cannot but bring about the ruin of Europe itself, and that Europe, if it is not careful, will perish from the void it has created around itself.[109]

Endnotes

1. HG Wells, *The War of the Worlds*, (Alma Classics, 2017), xx.
2. Duncan Bell, *Dreamworlds of Race: Empire and the Utopian Destiny of Anglo-America*, (Princeton University Pres, 2022), 190.
3. See Michael Taussig, *Shamanism, Colonialism, and the Wild Man: A Study in Terror and Healing* (University of Chicago Press, 1986).
4. Ursula Le Guin, "Rant about technology," Available online https://www.ursulakleguin.com/a-rant-about-technology, 2005.
5. Eve Tuck and K. Wayne Yang, Decolonization is not a Metaphor, Decolonization: indigineity, Education & Society Vol. 1, No. 1, 2012,pp.1–40, 7.
6. Ibid., 16.
7. T. Garba, & S Sorentino, "Slavery is a Metaphor: A Critical Commentary on Eve Tuck and K. Wayne Yang's "Decolonization is Not a Metaphor." (Antipode 2020). doi:10.1111/anti.12615. 2–3.
8. C. Hoene Jagadish Chandra Bose and the anticolonial politics of science fiction, "The Journal of Commonwealth Literature. (November 2020). doi:10.1177/0021989420966772
9. Though not extremophiles Tardigrades also often come up in such discussions (not an extremophile since they do not thrive in any of these particular extreme environments rather they are simply indifferent to them).
10. L. Billings, "Astrobiology in culture: the search for extraterrestrial life as 'science'", *Astrobiology*, Oct;12(10):966–75(2012).
11. Viveiros de Castro, Cannibal metaphysics: For a post-structural anthropology, (University of Minnesota Press, 2017), 50.
12. de Castro, *Cannibal Metaphysics*, 50–52.

[13] As Bernard Dionysius Geoghegan states in his book *Code: From Information Theory to French Theory* (Duke University Press, 2023), Levi-Strauss is of particular importance because we was swept up by but ultimately rejected the universalizing tendencies of anthropology particularly anthropological and ethnographic work that utilised cybernetics or systems theory to supposedly avoid problems of context and history (and the impacts of colonialism).

[14] Stefan Helmreich, "Extraterrestrial Relativism" *Anthropological Quarterly*, Vol. 85, No. 4, p. 1125–1140,

[15] Carl Sagan, *The Cosmic Connection: An Extraterrestrial Perspective* (Book Club, 1973), 46–47.

[16] Milan Ćirković, "Fermi's ParadoxThe Last Challenge for Copernicanism?,' Serbian Astronomical Journal 2009(178), 2009.

[17] Nick Bostrom, "Where are they?: Why I hope the search for intelligent life finds nothing" *MIT ?Technology Review*, May/June?issue:?pp. 72–77, (2008). The implosion of Bostrom's Future of Humanity Institute due to charges of eugenics should give us more than pause regarding pessimistic interpretations of alien life and many of the standard views of culture and civilisation from a decolonial perspective.

[18] Charlie Jane Anders, "The Fermi-Paradox is Our Business Model" *Reactor Mag*, 2010. Available Online https://reactormag.com/the-fermi-paradox-is-our-business-model/

[19] Liu Cixvin, The Dark Forest

[20] Cixin, Dark Forest, xxxx

[21] Liu Cixin, *The Dark Forest*, trans. Joel Martinsen, Tom Doherty Associates (Tor Books 2015), 503–507.

[22] Liu Cixin, "The Worst of All Possible Universes and the Best of All Possible Earths: Three Body and Chinese Science Fiction" *Reactor Mag*, 2014, available online https://reactormag.com/repost-the-worst-of-all-possible-

universes-and-the-best-of-all-possible-earths-three-body-and-chinese-science-fiction/
23 Mignola and Ye, "The Prospect of Harmony and the Decolonial View of the World: Weihua Ye Interviews Walter Mignolo", Marxism and Reality, no. 4, p.110–120. Shorter version Available Online https://criticallegalthinking.com/2014/06/12/prospect-harmony-decolonial-view-mignolo/
24 Ibid.
25 Jiayang Fan, "Liu Cixin's War of the Worlds," New Yorker Online 2019, Available Online https://www.newyorker.com/magazine/2019/06/24/liu-cixins-war-of-the-worlds
26 Ross Andersen, "What Happens if China Makes First Contact," The Atlantic, 2017. Available Online https://www.theatlantic.com/magazine/archive/2017/12/what-happens-if-china-makes-first-contact/544131/
27 Xin Fang, "Asian Futurism and the Non-Other," E-Flux, Issue #81 April 2017. Available Online https://www.e-flux.com/journal/81/126662/asian-futurism-and-the-non-other/
28 Yuk Hui "Cosmotechnics as Cosmopolitics" in E-Flux Issue Issue #86, November 2017
29 Georges Bataille, The Absence of Myth: Writings on Surrealism, trans. Michael Richardson, (Verso, 1994), 81.
30 RiversSolomon, Daveed Diggs, William Hutson, and Jonathan Snipes, The Deep. (Simon & Schuster. 2020)
31 David Scott "Antinomies of Slavery, Enlightenment, and Universal History" small axe 33 • November 2010, 162.
32 Frederick Douglass and Robert B Stepto. Narrative of the Life of Frederick Douglass, an American Slave. Cambridge, Ma: Belknap Press Of Harvard University Press, 2009, 78.
33 David Slade, (dir)American Gods Season 1 ep 2 "The Secret of Spoons, HBO Aired May 7, 2017
34 Gregoire Chamayou, Manhunts: A Philosophical History, (Princeton University Press, 2012).

35 Ryan Coogler, *Black Panther*, (Walt Disney Studios Motion Pictures, 2018).
36 Katherine McKittrick, *Dear Science and Other Stories* (Duke University Press, 2021), 50.
37 Nettrice R. Gaskins, "Deep Sea Dwellers - Drexciya and the Sonic Third Space" Scribd. Accessed July 9, 2024. https://www.scribd.com/document/375159110/Deep-Sea-Dwellers-Drexciya-and-the-Sonic-Third-Space-Nettrice-R-Gaskins
38 Blanck, Nili. 2022. "The Mesoamerican Influences behind Namor from 'Black Panther: Wakanda Forever.'" Smithsonian Magazine. November 10, 2022. https://www.smithsonianmag.com/history/the-mesoamerican-influences-behind-namor-from-black-panthewakanda-forever-180981106/
39 See Chapter 1 of Frantz Fanon, *Black Skin, White Masks*, (Pluto Press, 2017)
40 Sylvia Wynter, "Unsettling the Coloniality of Being/Power/Truth/Freedom: Towards the Human, after Man, Its Overrepresentation—an Argument." CR The New Centennial Review (2003) 3 (3): 257–337. https://doi.org/10.1353/ncr.2004.0015.
41 Amanda Dominguez-Chio, "District 9—A Post-Colonial Analysis," *The Artifice,* 2014. Available Online https://the-artifice.com/district-9-post-colonial-analysis/
42 John Rieder, *Colonialism and the Emergence of Science Fiction*, (Wesleyan, 2012),106.
43 Darwin, The Descent of Man
44 Patrick Lin, Keith Abney, and George A. Bekey, *Robot Ethics: The Ethical and Social Implications of Robotics*, (The MIT Press, 2011).
45 Joanna J. Bryson, "Robots should be slaves" in Yorick Wilks (ed.), Close Engagements with Artificial Companions: Key social, psychological, ethical and design issues. John Benjamins Publishing. pp. 63–74 (2010).

46. Zakiyyah Iman Jackson, *Becoming Human: Matter and Meaning in an Antiblack World*, (New York University Press, 2020), 5.
47. Ibid., 25.
48. Roxanne Dunbar Ortiz, *An Indigenous Peoples History of the United States*, (Beacon Press, 2015), 99.
49. See Gloria Anzaldua, *Borderlands/La Frontera: The New Mestiza*, 1987.
50. This is discussed at length in Wynter's work particularly in essays from the late 1980s.
51. Michael Sheyahshe (January 2008). "Native Resolution". Games for Windows: The Official Magazine (14): 32.
52. Kim Tallbear. "Who Owns the Ancient One?" BuzzFeed News, July 3, 2015. https://www.buzzfeednews.com/article/kimtallbear/how-the-man-stole-ancient-man-from-his-native-descendents.
53. Though Dussell does not mention that Las Casas suggests using African slaves instead.
54. Aimee Bahng, *Migrant Futures: Decolonizing Speculation in Financial Times*, (Duke University Press, 2018), 54.
55. Ibid., 75.
56. There is also an entire slew of brain or mind replacement stories with racist overtones. Jordan Peele's *Get Out* pushes back against these. One of the most notorious is Robert Heinlein's *See No Evil* in which a rich white man transplants his brain into a young Black woman and ends up impregnating 'his' new body with 'his' old sperm.
57. Nick Estes, *Our History Is the Future: Standing Rock Versus the Dakota Access Pipeline, and the Long Tradition of Indigenous Resistance*, 19–20.
58. We could go even further into Weird West and Western Horror such as *Highplanes Invaders* and *The Burrowers*.
59. Estes, *Our History Is the Future*, 69.

60 See the introduction to Huang, Betsy, and Greta A. Niu, *Techno-Orientalism: Imagining Asia in Speculative Fiction, History, and Media,* (Rutgers University Press, 2015).

61 The success of *Everything Everywhere all at Once* seems to be a potentially interesting response in celebrating Chinese-American identity and utilizing the multiverse to do it. However despite breaking many representational barriers in Hollywood the ultimate message of the film (your worst life is still worth living) seems deeply revisionary and liberal in the thinnest sense of the word.

62 To be fair to Villienueve however it should be noted that his film only covers the first half of the first book.

63 David M. Higgins, "Psychic Decolonization in 1960s Science Fiction." *Science Fiction Studies*, Vol. 40, No. 2 (July 2013): 228-245.

64 IBRAHIM AL MARASHI, "The film 'Dune', techno-Orientalism, and intergalactic Islam" *Trt World,* 2021, Available Online, https://www.trtworld.com/opinion/the-film-dune-techno-orientalism-and-intergalactic-islam-52273

65 Michael Berry, ""Dune," climate fiction pioneer: The ecological lessons of Frank Herbert's sci-fi masterpiece were ahead of its time" *Salon.com,* Available Online https://www.salon.com/2015/08/13/dune_climate_fiction_pioneer_the_ecological_lessons_of_frank_herberts_sci_fi _masterpiece_were_ahead_of_its_time

66 Edward Said, *Orientalism*, (Penguin Classics, 2003), 4.

67 Liang Luscombe, "Tired of the Future: Techno-Orientalism and the Trappings of Speculative World Building," *Liminal Mag,* (Online, 2022) Available https://www.liminalmag.com/mirror/tired-of-the-future

68 Hee-Jung S. Joo 'The Asian (as) Robot: Queer Inhumans in the Works of Margaret Rhee, Greg Pak, and Chang-Rae Lee,' *Journal of Asian American Studies* 25, no. 1 (2022): 1–30

69. See Aysha, Emad El-Din. "Science Fiction by, about, and for Arabs: Case Studies in De-Orientalising the Western Imagination." ReOrient 6, no. 1 (2020): 4–19.
70. Said, *Orientalism*, 59.
71. Ibid., 252.
72. Ibid., 98–100.
73. Abdel-Halim, Amina. 2023. "Between Resistance and Heritage: Science Fiction in the Arab World." Egyptian Streets. February 12, 2023. https://egyptianstreets.com/2023/02/12/between-resistance-and-heritage-arab-science-fiction/.
74. Ibid.
75. C. Hoffmann, "Environmental determinism as Orientalism: The geopolitical ecology of crisis in the Middle East," *J Hist Sociol*. 2018;31:94–104.
76. Kristen Alvanson's *XYZT* (Urbanomic, 2019) plays on the supposedly clear lines of a West and an Orientalist West by having magic and technology consume one another. The novel tells of teleporting peoples eroding any Orientalist pretext.
77. Amitav Ghosh, *The Nutmeg's Curse: Parables for a Planet in Crisis*, (Penguin, 2021). 52–53.
78. Dian K Davis, "Introduction," to *Environmental Imagines of the Middle East and North Africa*, Ed. Diana K. Davis and Edmund Burke III, (Ohio University Press, 2011).
79. Elana Gomel, *Science Fiction, Alien Encounters, and the Ethics of Posthumanism: Beyond the Golden Rule*, (Palgrave Macmillan, 2014), 117.
80. Ibid.
81. Ibid., 119.
82. On this see Tia Trafford, *The Empire at Home: Internal Colonies and the End of Britain*, (Pluto Press, 2020)
83. Suparno Banerjee, *Indian Science Fiction: Patterns, History and Hybridity*, (University of Wales Press, 2020), 21.

84 There is also the peculiar layered bio-mimicry present in wealthy Western women in the 1800s who appropriated Indian dresses and designs that used beetle wing castings as decoration. See Kenna Libes, "Glory in a Host of Entomological Spoils" Beetle-Wing Embroidery and the Exhibition of India in Anglo-American Dress, 1780–1903.

85 There are more incidental or at least less overtly speculative forms such as the father figure in Arundhati Roy's *The God of Small Things*. See Catherine PESSO-MIQUEL, "Breaking Bounds in Arundhati Roy's The God of Small Things ", La Clé des Langues [en ligne], Lyon, ENS de LYON/DGESCO (ISSN 2107-7029), mai 2011. Consulté le 11/07/2024. URL: https://cle.ens-lyon.fr/anglais/litterature/litterature-postcoloniale/dossier-the-god-of-small-things/breaking-bounds-in-arundhati-roy-s-the-god-of-small-things

86 Oliver Cox, *Caste, Class, and Race,* (Monthly Review Press, 1948), 439.

87 In Lindsay Ellis *Axiom's End* (St Martins Press, 2020) there is a first contact scenario in which the protagonist has to deal with the sheer difference of an insectoid species. But in the novel there is an explicit connection made between the inevitability of violence and the species being biologically bound to an insect-like system of hierarchical difference.

88 It is also worth noting how in *Starship Troopers* Robert Heinlein says that the giant bugs of the planet Klandathu can be communist because they (as insects) are perfectly evolved to be that way.

89 Charlotte Sleigh (2001) "Empire Of The Ants: H.G. Wells and Tropical Entomology, Science as Culture", 10:1, 33–71.

90 Ibid., 55.

92 Anmoi Serfan, "The Making of Pakistani Sci-Fi How Pakistan's artists are reinventing the genre to subvert their own status quo" *Newline Magazine,* (Online, 2021) Available

online https://newlinesmag.com/reportage/the-making-of-pakistani-sci-fi/

93 In a very different vein there is the Baliwood musical *Koi... Mil Gaya* (*I Have Found Someone*) in which a mentally disabled man befriends an alien which allows for some external perspective to ridicule certain formalisms of Indian culture.

94 Nudrat Kamal, "What South Asian Sci-Fi Can Tell Us About Our World" *The Wire*, (Online, 2019), Available Online https://thewire.in/culture/what-south-asian-sci-fi-can-tell-us-about-our-world

95 Ibid.

96 Hoene C. Jagadish "Chandra Bose and the anticolonial politics of science fiction," The Journal of Commonwealth Literature. November 2020.

97 Arthur C. Clarke , "Clarke's Third Law on UFO's," *Science* v. 159 (1968), 255–255.

98 Wynter, "Unsettling Coloniality," 297.

99 Ibid., 309–310.

100 Kim Tallbear, "DNA, Blood, and Racializing the Tribe", *Wicazo Sa Review* Vol. 18, No. 1 (Spring, 2003), pp. 81–107, 84.

101 Steven Pinker, "Why nature & nurture won't go away." *Daedalus* 133(4): 5–17, (2004) 11.

102 Genealogy, Epistemology and Worldmaking Amia Srinivasan, Proceedings of the Aristotelian Society 119 (2):127–156 (2019)

103 Kyle Whyte, "Indigenous Science (Fiction) for the Anthropocene: Ancestral Dystopias and Fantasies of Climate Change Crises" 226

104 Crary, Alice "The Horrific History of Comparisons between Cognitive Disability and Animality (and How to Move Past it),"

105 Kim Tallbear, *Native American DNA: Tribal Belonging and the False Promise of Genetic Science*, (University of Minnesota Press, 2013), 204.
106 Sylvia Wynter, 'Afterword: Beyond Miranda's Meanings: Un/Silencing the "Demonic Ground" of Caliban's "Woman"', in *Out of the Kumbla: Caribbean Women and Literature*, ed. Carole Boyce Davies and Elaine Savory (Trenton: Africa World Press, 1990), 358.
107 Percy Shelley(as Marlow) Preface to Shelley, Mary. 2022. *Frankenstein, or the Modern Prometheus*, Milne Press Online (1818 Edition). Available online https://milnepublishing.geneseo.edu/suny-corningcc-frankenstein/front-matter/preface/
108 See also Lewis Gordon, "Decolonializing Frankenstein." Common Reader. The Common Reader. October 27, 2018. https://commonreader.wustl.edu/c/decolonializing-frankenstein/.
109 Aimé Césaire, *Discourse on Colonialism*, Monthly Review Press, 2000), 74–75.

CULTURE, SOCIETY, & POLITICS

Contemporary culture has eliminated the concept and public figure of the intellectual. A cretinous anti-intellectualism presides, cheer-led by hacks in the pay of multinational corporations who reassure their bored readers that there is no need to rouse themselves from their stupor. Zer0 Books knows that another kind of discourse—intellectual without being academic, popular without being populist—is not only possible but already flourishing. Zer0 is convinced that in the unthinking, blandly consensual culture in which we live, critical and engaged theoretical reflection is more important
than ever before.
If you have enjoyed this book, why not tell other readers by posting a review on your preferred book site.
You may also wish to
subscribe to our Zer0 Books YouTube Channel.

Bestsellers from Zer0 Books include:

Poor but Sexy
Culture Clashes in Europe East and West
Agata Pyzik
How the East stayed East and the West stayed West.
Paperback:978-1-78099-394-2 ebook: 978-1-78099-395-9

An Anthropology of Nothing in Particular
Martin Demant Frederiksen
A journey into the social lives of meaninglessness.
Paperback: 978-1-78535-699-5 ebook: 978-1-78535-700-8

In the Dust of This Planet
Horror of Philosophy vol. 1
Eugene Thacker
In the first of a series of three books on the Horror of Philosophy, *In the Dust of This Planet* offers the genre of horror as a way of thinking about the unthinkable.
Paperback: 978-1-84694-676-9 ebook: 978-1-78099-010-1

The End of Oulipo?
An Attempt to Exhaust a Movement
Lauren Elkin, Veronica Esposito
Paperback: 978-1-78099-655-4 ebook: 978-1-78099-656-1

Capitalist Realism
Is There No Alternative?
Mark Fisher
An analysis of the ways in which capitalism has presented itself
as the only realistic political-economic system.
Paperback: 978-1-84694-317-1 ebook: 978-1-78099-734-6

Rebel Rebel
Chris O'Leary
David Bowie: every single song. Everything you want to know,
everything you didn't know.
Paperback: 978-1-78099-244-0 ebook: 978-1-78099-713-1

Cartographies of the Absolute
Alberto Toscano, Jeff Kinkle
An aesthetics of the economy for the twenty-first century.
Paperback: 978-1-78099-275-4 ebook: 978-1-78279-973-3

Malign Velocities
Accelerationism and Capitalism
Benjamin Noys
Long-listed for the Bread and Roses Prize 2015, *Malign Velocities*
argues against the need for speed, tracking acceleration
as the symptom of the ongoing crises of capitalism.
Paperback: 978-1-78279-300-7 ebook: 978-1-78279-299-4

Babbling Corpse
Vaporwave and the Commodification of Ghosts
Grafton Tanner
Paperback: 978-1-78279-759-3 ebook: 978-1-78279-760-9

New Work New Culture
Work we want and a culture that strengthens us
Frithjof Bergmann
A serious alternative for humankind and the planet.
Paperback: 978-1-78904-064-7 ebook: 978-1-78904-065-4

Romeo and Juliet in Palestine
Teaching Under Occupation
Tom Sperlinger
Life in the West Bank, the nature of pedagogy, and the role of a university under occupation.
Paperback: 978-1-78279-637-4 ebook: 978-1-78279-636-7

Color, Facture, Art and Design
Iona Singh
This materialist definition of fine art develops guidelines for architecture, design, cultural studies, and ultimately, social change.
Paperback: 978-1-78099-629-5 ebook: 978-1-78099-630-1

Sweetening the Pill
or How We Got Hooked on Hormonal Birth Control
Holly Grigg-Spall
Has contraception liberated or oppressed women?
Sweetening the Pill breaks the silence on the dark side of hormonal contraception.
Paperback: 978-1-78099-607-3 ebook: 978-1-78099-608-0

Why Are We the Good Guys?
Reclaiming Your Mind from the Delusions of Propaganda
David Cromwell
A provocative challenge to the standard ideology that Western power is a benevolent force in the world.
Paperback: 978-1-78099-365-2 ebook: 978-1-78099-366-9

The Writing on the Wall
On the Decomposition of Capitalism and its Critics
Anselm Jappe, Alastair Hemmens
A new approach to the meaning of social emancipation.
Paperback: 978-1-78535-581-3 ebook: 978-1-78535-582-0

Neglected or Misunderstood
The Radical Feminism of Shulamith Firestone
Victoria Margree
An interrogation of issues surrounding gender, biology, sexuality, work, and technology, and the ways in which our imaginations continue to be in thrall to ideologies of maternity and the nuclear family.
Paperback: 978-1-78535-539-4 ebook: 978-1-78535-540-0

How to Dismantle the NHS in 10 Easy Steps
(Second Edition)
Youssef El-Gingihy
The story of how your NHS was sold off and why you will have to buy private health insurance soon. A new expanded second edition with chapters on junior doctors' strikes and government blueprints for US-style healthcare.
Paperback: 978-1-78904-178-1 ebook: 978-1-78904-179-8

Digesting Recipes
The Art of Culinary Notation
Susannah Worth
A recipe is an instruction, the imperative tone of the expert, but this constraint can offer its own kind of potential. A recipe need not be a domestic trap but might instead offer escape—something to fantasise about or aspire to.
Paperback: 978-1-78279-860-6 ebook: 978-1-78279-859-0

Most titles are published in paperback and as an ebook. Paperbacks are available in traditional bookshops. Both print and ebook formats are available online.
Follow us at:
https://www.facebook.com/ZeroBooks
https://twitter.com/Zer0Books
https://www.instagram.com/zero.books

For video content, author interviews, and more, please subscribe to our YouTube channel:

zer0repeater

Follow us on social media for book news, promotions, and more:

Facebook: ZeroBooks

Instagram: @zero.books

X: @Zer0Books

Tik Tok: @zer0repeater